The Volvo's bumper was caved in. Buffy struck her head against the driver's side window as the car rolled toward the tree line, and for a moment, she was unconscious.

When her eyes peeled open and she looked out through the shattered glass, she saw steel and fiberglass carnage. The Kakchiquels seemed stunned for a moment, as though they had no idea how to proceed.

Then, among them, Buffy saw a pale, ravenhaired creature rise up, gossamer gown fluttering around her.

Drusilla.

Her chest hurt with every breath, but Buffy built a wall between herself and that pain. There was no time for it. With the shouts of the vampires in her ears, she released her seat belt and lunged for the door. Her fingers closed around the latch and she tried to pop it open.

It was jammed shut from the crash.

"Smell her, puppies!" Drusilla cried in a singsong voice, hoarse with desire. "Like cinnamon and nutmeg. A fox hunt, now! A taste of her boldness to the first to make her scream!

"But save the eyes for me."

Buffy the Vampire Slayer™

Available from ARCHWAY Paperbacks and Pocket Pulse

Available from POCKET BOOKS

Buffy
the vampire slayer™

THE LOST SLAYER

Part Two

DARK TIMES

CHRISTOPHER GOLDEN

**An original serial novel based on the hit TV series
created by Joss Whedon**

POCKET PULSE

New York   London   Toronto   Sydney   Singapore

For information regarding special discounts for bulk purchases, please contact Simon & Schuster Special Sales at 1-800-456-6798 or business@simonandschuster.com

HISTORIAN'S NOTE: This serial story takes place at the beginning of *Buffy*'s fourth season.

This book is a work of fiction. Names, characters, places and incidents are products of the author's imagination or are used fictitiously. Any resemblance to actual events or locales or persons, living or dead, is entirely coincidental.

An *Original* Publication of POCKET BOOKS

 POCKET PULSE, published by
Pocket Books, a division of Simon & Schuster, Inc.
1230 Avenue of the Americas, New York, NY 10020

ISBN: 0-7434-1186-2

First Pocket Pulse printing September 2001

10 9 8 7 6 5 4 3 2 1

POCKET PULSE and colophon are registered trademarks of Simon & Schuster, Inc.

Printed in the U.S.A.

PROLOGUE

*T*orn away.

Buffy hurtled forward, not propelled from behind but tugged, dragged, hauled painfully and suddenly into a black and red abyss. It felt as though only her face had been torn away, pulled on farther and farther into the chasm of infinite black before her, but the rest of her left behind, all the weight that flesh and blood and bone added to the image she had of herself. What was she? Mind and heart and soul. Face. Eyes and ears and mouth. Words.

Red whirlpools punctured the endless velvet shadow around her, flashing past as she was dragged by. As if the universe itself were wounded and bleeding.

Vaguely, in the fog that seemed to comprise her mind, a dark certainty overwhelmed her.

This was not a vision. Somehow, her spirit had been torn from her body and was now on a journey. Traveling. Hurtling out of control toward some unfathomable point in the distance.

Buffy felt her mind slipping away from her, felt herself shutting down as she was drawn through the void . . . and drawn . . . and drawn. Lulled into a kind of hibernation, aware and yet unresponsive to her surroundings.

Then, suddenly, some sense that the void was not endless, the abyss not infinite. Somewhere ahead was a barrier, a wall, and she was hurtling toward it, bound for collision. She peered into the darkness ahead but all had become black now, as though she were blind. But blind or not, she could feel it, sense its proximity as she was whipped along a course toward inevitable impact.

Collision.

Cold water splashed her face.

Shocked, Buffy stared at her fingers, splayed before her. At the grimy, cracked porcelain of the sink and the water running from the faucet. Instinctively she looked up for a mirror over the sink, but there wasn't one.

Of course there isn't one. They took it away the first day, she thought. She flashed back to that time, five years before, when Clownface and Bulldog had thrown her, beaten, bloody and barely conscious, into this cell for the first time. *They didn't want you to cut your wrists.*

Buffy spun about like a cornered animal, and her eyes darted around the room. The cell. Bars on the two high windows barely allowed the tiniest bit of light from the outside. Ten-foot stone walls all around. A steel door with rivets driven through it and neither handle nor knob nor even keyhole on this side.

Built for me. This was built for me.

Her hands went to the sides of her head and she squeezed her eyes closed. Then she opened them wide and gazed around the room, hugging herself tight. Buffy knew things. She did not know how, but she *knew.*

Impossible.

But inescapably true.

She had been here, in this cell, for a very long time. Reluctantly, afraid of what she would find, she looked at her hands again. Rough, hard hands, with lines that had never been there before. She stretched, felt her body, *looked* at herself.

No thinner than before. But harder. Tighter. Rippled with muscles she remembered seeing in magazines and on television whenever they showed women who were Olympians, whose very life was exercise, exertion, sport.

But there was nothing sporting about this.

Buffy's body was taut and dangerous. She felt it, even in the way she moved. She felt like a weapon.

Gathering dust.

This cell. Endless days and nights alone, with only

these four walls and the ruthless way she forged her body into this steel thing. Vampires with tattooed faces and orange flames in their eyes; they fed her, kept her alive, but nothing more. No talking, not even threats or taunts. Only the toning of her body kept her sane, that focus on the day she would escape.

And in time, even that focus blurred and there was only the routine of exercise. Hope dimmed.

These aren't my memories. Can't be my memories. I remember yesterday. They took Giles. Camazotz is preying on Sunnydale. Lucy Hanover came in my dreams and Willow summoned her and . . .

Buffy stared down at her hands again. And they *were* her hands. Just as the memories of this room— month after month becoming intimate with these four walls, eating the awful slop they fed her, and waiting for an opening—just as those recollections were hers.

Lines on her hands.

Five years since she had been put into this room.

"No," she whispered. *It's impossible.*

"No!" she screamed.

With a roar of fury and hatred surging up from her chest, Buffy ran full tilt at the door. Though her body still felt foreign to her, she loved the way it moved. Fluid and powerful and deadly. She launched a drop kick at the steel door, slammed into it hard enough to rattle her jaw, then fell and banged her head hard on the stone floor. Adrenaline screamed in her, and she pushed the pain away. With a flip, she was up on her feet, and she kicked and punched at the door with only the echo of her own grunts in the room to accompany her.

Several minutes passed. She slowed, breathing heavily.

The adrenaline subsided. The ache in her skull and the pain in her bloody, ravaged knuckles was real. The skin on her fists was scraped raw. Buffy reached up to touch the back of her head, where she'd struck the floor, and her fingers came back streaked with blood.

She would heal quickly. After all, she was the Slayer. But the wounds were real. This was real.

Even as her mind recoiled in horror at these thoughts, even as she examined her body and her surroundings, she felt her memory of the battle with Camazotz begin to dim. Desperate to save Giles, they had summoned Lucy Hanover. Lucy had called upon an entity known only as The Prophet, who promised Buffy a vision of the future, a vision that might help her prevent it and save Giles's life.

The Prophet had touched her.

But this was no vision.

Whatever The Prophet had done, somehow she was not nineteen anymore. Buffy Summers was twenty-four, at least. Maybe twenty-five. Somehow, the entity had torn her spirit from her body that day, years ago, and thrust it into the future, into this body.

Her memories of that day faded, now. Though she

knew in her heart that in some way it had happened only moments before, she remembered it as though years had passed. But there was a blank spot there as well—a period of days she did not remember at all— the time during which she had been captured. A gap in her memory existed between The Prophet touching her and the day when Clownface and Bulldog threw her into her cell.

For more than five years, she had wondered what had happened in that dead space in her memory, that blackout.

No. It isn't me. I haven't been here. It never happened, she reminded herself. And yet there was no longer any doubt that this was real. She could feel every muscle, every scratch, every sensation. This was her own body, her own life, and yet somehow her nineteen-year-old mind had been fast-forwarded into an older body, a dark, horrible future.

And all she could do was pace the cell. Work her body. Train for the day the vampires let their guard down.

Days passed. She trained and slept and washed and trained. They brought food before dawn and after dusk, always armed, always in groups of three or more. Made her stand in the far corner, afraid to have her come too close, as though she were a wild animal.

It made her smile.

Perhaps two weeks later, they brought the girl.

It was dark when they threw her into the cell,

bruised and bloody but conscious. Alive. The girl was a brunette, dark and exotic. *Italian, maybe,* Buffy thought. Tall, but young. Even through the blood, when she looked up with her defiant, crazy eyes, Buffy could see that she was just a kid. Not more than sixteen, maybe younger.

For a moment, Buffy only stood there staring at her, five years without human contact having built up a callus on her heart and soul. She was two people in one, two Buffys at one time, the hardened prisoner and the young warrior. Then suddenly it was as though the part of her mind that was still nineteen simply woke up. It was as though she had been frozen in this body from the moment she had realized what had happened to her.

Now she thawed.

Ice melted away from her true self.

Buffy went to the girl, reached down for her. "Are you all right?"

The girl's eyes changed then. She blinked and her mouth opened with an expression of absolute astonishment.

"Oh my God," the girl whispered, voice cracking. "You're . . . you're her, aren't you?"

"I'm not tracking."

The girl backed away, stood up slowly, painfully, and stared at her. "You're Buffy Summers. I've seen pictures."

"Yeah? How do I look?"

Beaten, bleeding, the girl actually laughed. A discordant sound, but a welcome one just the same. "Like hell," she said. "You look like hell."

"Who are you?" Buffy asked.

But she thought she already knew the answer.

"I'm August."

Buffy frowned. "You're a month?"

"It's my name," the girl said, annoyed. She wiped blood from under her nose but it was still bleeding. "I'm the Slayer now."

Buffy closed her eyes. Shook her head to clear her mind. She felt a little unsteady on her feet. So many questions. But if this girl was a Slayer, what did that mean for—

"Faith?"

August nodded. "Six months ago. They tried for years to catch her, the way they . . . the way they did you. If it weren't for her they'd have the whole West Coast by now, maybe more. At least that's what my Watcher says. They caught her outside of L.A., I heard."

Wary, maybe even a little afraid, the girl gave Buffy a cautious look. "Have you been here all along? All this time?"

No. I just got here. A couple of weeks ago. I'm not supposed to be here. Those were the first thoughts in her head, but even as they flickered through her mind she knew they weren't really true.

"All this time," Buffy told her. She turned her back on the girl and began to pace the room. "And now I've got company."

"But haven't you tried to—"

Buffy spun to face her, nearly growling. "Every day. What the hell do you think I am? I'm the Slayer."

"You're *a* Slayer," August corrected. "Not even the main one anymore. Not for a long time. The Council, they just call you the Lost Slayer now. Not even your name."

Buffy took that in. In her mind she reached back to the moment she knew was truly hers, where her mind belonged. Her soul . . . where her soul had been pushed away, into the here and now, and her body left behind. Hijacked.

What had happened between then and now? Where were they all? What had happened to Giles?

"How much territory do they control? Camazotz and the vampires?" she asked.

August seemed deeply troubled. She stared at the steel door, then turned back to look at Buffy, sizing her up.

"Well?" Buffy prodded.

"Sunnydale. A few other ~~t~~ ... ~~ybe~~ a thirty mile radius around."

"And nobod~~~~"

"No~~~~ ... ~~s~~," August told her. "Nobody wants ~~~~ ~~that~~'s how they win. Spin control. Market-~~s~~ ~~the~~ illusion that everything's normal. Plenty of humans willing to help for a piece of the power."

"God," Buffy rasped.

"So there's no way out of here?" August asked, her voice taking on a kind of quiet desperation, as if she had surrendered a part of herself. "You've tried everything?"

"Five years is a long time," Buffy told her. "Maybe with two of us now it'll be different, but I figure they'll just send more guards now to bring the meals."

"Then I guess we don't have any choice," August said softly. Her eyes filled with moisture and she wiped at them bitterly. Then she took a breath and steadied herself, a grim expression on her face.

"Again, not tracking," Buffy told her.

August stared at her as though she were stupid. "They captured you because they finally got smart. If you don't kill the Slayer, there won't be another one. Keep you in here . . ." she whirled around, threw her arms up in near hysteria. "Keep us in here, and there'll never be another Slayer."

Buffy stared at her. "You have a gift for stating the obvious."

"You're just going to let them? There's nothing to stop them from spreading even further now." August bit her lip, shook her head and hugged herself as though attempting to deny the thoughts that were filling her head.

"It sucks. It truly does," Buffy said, hearing the pain in her own voice. The despair. "But until they get careless, and let down their guard, there's nothing we can do."

August pushed a lock of her dark hair behind her ears. She would not turn her iron-gray eyes up to look at Buffy.

"There's something I can do," she said softly.

One eyebrow raised, Buffy studied her. "What's that? What can you do?"

Finally, August met her gaze. Her soft eyes had hardened again. Crazy, defiant eyes. Eyes cold and decisive.

"I can kill you."

CHAPTER 1

I can kill you.

The stone walls of the cell echoed back the words, and then silence descended. No noise came from the corridor beyond the steel door. The only thing Buffy Summers could hear was her own gentle breathing, and that of the sixteen-year-old girl standing across from her. The one who had spoken those impossible words.

Buffy tensed, taut muscles bunched, and she rose on the balls of her feet. Five years she had been in this fifteen-foot square, a chamber of rock and metal constructed with the express purpose of keeping her within. Five years she had honed her body until it was a coiled spring, a scalpel, a bullwhip . . . all of that and more. When the vampires came to bring food or clothing or bedding, they came in force, with stun guns, and they used them. In all the times she had tried to escape and failed, all the dreams she had had of combat, never had she imagined that the next threat she would face would come from another Slayer.

The girl, August, sensed the alarm in Buffy, and her stance altered slightly, subtly. Though younger, the dark-haired girl was taller than Buffy, and likely thought that an advantage.

"You're not thinking clearly," Buffy said, a rasp in her voice. She had used it so little in recent years.

August seemed to quiver, almost humming with energy like a high-tension wire. Her tongue snaked out and wetted her lips. "My thinking is perfectly clear, Summers. It's your head that's not screwed on straight here. Look around. You're a zoo animal. They've kept you like a tiger in a cage, and you've *let* them."

Again, her words echoed off cold stone. The two young women began, slowly, to move, to circle, eyeing one another, looking for vulnerabilities. In the back of her mind, a voice shouted for Buffy to stop this madness, not to let it happen. It was the voice of her younger self, somehow implanted within this twenty-four-year-old body. But the two minds were both *her*, and so they had begun to merge. The two were one. Despite the reluctance she felt, Buffy knew that only a fool would leave herself open to attack.

It was simple caution for her to be wary of August's threat. The girl, the young Slayer, had a desperation in her eyes that said she might do anything.

"For more than three years, I tried to escape every time the door was opened," Buffy said. "They took to stunning me on principle. After a while I decided to study them instead, try to figure out the psychology of my jailers. Within six months I knew them all, their vulnerabilities, what would work to distract them. Just from listening and watching. Two days before I planned to make my escape, they were all replaced. Someone knew. Someone understood what I was doing."

"Exactly my point," August said grimly. She shook her hands out as she glared at Buffy. "You're a pet. Your master knows you too well."

Buffy froze. "I don't have a master."

"Look around. They might as well have one of those little hamster wheels in here. Or a Habitrail."

Buffy stepped slightly back from August and kept the girl in her peripheral vision, then did indeed look around. Though the room was cold stone, there were several throw rugs on the floor. A plastic rack upon which were piled the blue jeans, white tanks, and sweatshirts they supplied her with; all U.C. Sunnydale sweatshirts, which were all the vampires would give her. Some kind of joke, she was sure. There was her metal-framed bed—all welded to keep her from using part of it as a weapon, and a steel table bolted to the floor. Nothing wood, of course, for wood could splinter, and splintered wood could kill her captors.

"I don't see what you see. They need me alive," Buffy said. "Food and water, clothing."

August shook her head. The expression on her face might have been called a sneer if not for the sadness in it.

"All this time, though. If you realized that you couldn't escape, you could have found a way to force them to kill you. Could have killed yourself, if that didn't work. Shatter that porcelain sink, use it to slash your wrists, bleed out here on the floor. But you didn't. Why didn't you?"

Buffy shook her head. *"That's* your solution? What's the Council teaching you? I'm the Slayer. Once I get out, there'll be hell to pay."

Though she had been on guard, the absurdity of August's rantings had caused Buffy to pause for a moment in surprise.

August moved. With a single, fluid motion, so fast Buffy barely had time to react, she stepped into the space between them and lashed out with a savage backhand. The blow struck Buffy's cheek hard, but she rolled with it, turned in an instant and readied herself for another attack.

None came.

Instead, August only stood and stared at her, face reddened with rage. Tears began to stream down her face.

"How can you be so arrogant?" August demanded. A lock of her hair had fallen across her eyes but she did not move it. "You're *a* Slayer, not *the* Slayer. You're not what's important. The only thing that matters is that there be someone out there to fight them.

Once you get out, there'll be hell to pay? That's what you said. It's *already* hell out there, Summers. Can you help them?"

A chill seemed to weave frozen tendrils all through Buffy's body. Though the idea horrified her—everything August was suggesting did—there was a kind of blunt, primitive truth to it as well. Was it arrogant of her to think she was more valuable alive than dead? Simply by staying alive, she had given her captors what they wanted. Yet the idea of doing anything else . . .

She shook her head. "No. Listen. Now that we're both in here, we'll find a way. Before they figure out what it takes to contain us both."

August laughed bitterly and wiped away a tear. "You've been here five years! We can't get out, Buffy. The only way for there to be a new Slayer, out there, fighting the darkness, is for one of us to die. If you're not willing to do what has to be done . . . I will."

The dry shuffle of their feet upon the stone floor was an eerie whisper. The two Slayers began to circle again, and though she rejected the very idea of what was happening, Buffy could not deny it. It was a dark, vicious irony, a nightmare made real. Her throat was dry, but she felt the power in her body, tendons and muscles moving with grace and precision.

"I won't kill you, August. But I'm not going to let you kill me, either."

The girl's face darkened further. Fresh tears sprang to her cheeks. The teenager beneath the Slayer's façade was revealed.

"Damn you!" August cried, the words heavy with the weight of her pain and grief. "Do you think I want this? I've got people I love out there. Dying every day, trying to keep the vampires from spreading. Someone's got to protect them."

"We'll find a way. It may take a little time—"

But the conversation was over. August glared at her coldly, now, and wiped the last tear from her red-rimmed eyes. Her lips were pressed together in anguish, and she shuddered once, then was still. The girl dropped into a battle stance that Buffy was all too familiar with. It had been the first one Giles had taught her when he took over as her Watcher.

"August—"

"Quiet," the girl snapped.

August leaped at her in a spinning kick aimed directly at her head. Though Buffy saw it coming, had been prepared for it, it was only instinct that saved her from the blow. She darted her head to the side, dodged the kick by a scant half-inch. With her right hand, she caught August's ankle and reversed the direction of the kick, spinning the girl onto the floor. August's shoulder struck the stone hard, but even as Buffy moved in on her, the girl rolled, swung her foot out and swept Buffy's legs out from under her.

Even as she fell, Buffy spun and threw her body forward. She ducked her head, went into a roll that took her across the room, then leaped to her feet only inches shy of her bed.

August was already there. As Buffy came up, the

younger Slayer snapped a side kick at her chest. Buffy could not avoid it. Something in her chest cracked and all the breath went from her lungs. She crashed into the plastic shelving holding her clothes and it splintered and broke apart beneath her.

Her rib cage grated painfully as she moved, but Buffy rolled up against the wall, amidst the wreckage of the shelves. A shard of plastic pierced her side, but she ignored the lancing pain, so superficial compared to the burning in her chest when she breathed.

Mouth still set in that grim line, eyes red with tears fallen and unfallen, August went for a simple kick. Buffy had counted on her believing that her chest injury had caused her to cower against the wall to make herself less vulnerable. August was young. She bought it.

With an open hand, she stopped the kick mid-swing and shoved August backward. Braced against the wall, Buffy had enough support to knock her off her feet. With the enhanced strength of the Slayer, she pushed the younger Slayer with such force that August flailed at the air, unable to spin out of the fall. Her head struck the edge of the steel table as she went down.

Though she pushed herself up on her hands and knees, August was too slow, too vulnerable.

Buffy was up, frustrated, searching for some way to stop this fight before it ended the way August wanted it to.

She was stronger than this girl. Probably faster as well. August had been Slayer for six months, maybe trained for a year or two before that. Buffy had been the Slayer more than three years before she was captured and had worked her body mercilessly in the interim, not merely with exercise, but with shadow-boxing and a martial arts *kata* she had devised from the various disciplines she had studied before.

But she was trying to reason with a girl on the brink of madness, a Slayer driven past rationality by the world she lived in. It disturbed Buffy deeply to think how desperate things must be to drive August to this.

Not that it mattered, now.

The girl wanted to kill her. In order to prevent that, to reason with her, she would have to incapacitate the younger Slayer, at the very least.

She watched August warily, her eyes wide, imploring. "It shouldn't be like this."

August shook off the blow to her head. She would not raise her eyes to look at Buffy, only crouched there for a moment on hands and knees.

"No. It shouldn't," she agreed. "But it is."

Silent, lightning fast, August shot up from the floor and barreled into Buffy. It was a brute's move, with no finesse, no precision, but it worked. August used her greater height and weight to ram Buffy up against the stone wall. The impact drove the air from Buffy's lungs again, and the fire of pain in her chest from her cracked ribs flared even more brightly.

August snapped her open hand forward in a palm strike that drove into Buffy's shoulder quite precisely, dislocating it with a loud pop and an agonizing tear. Black spots clouded Buffy's vision, but she knew that was just the pain.

Pain was an old and familiar friend, by now.

It woke her up.

It pissed her off.

But before she could react, August gave her a quick shot to the face. Her nose broke and blood began to flow.

The next blow never touched her. Buffy dodged and August's fist hit the stone wall. Something in her hand broke with an audible snap, but August only grunted softly.

"That's it. You don't get any more free shots," Buffy snarled.

The copper tang of blood touched her lips, her dislocated arm hung loosely at her side, but Buffy popped August with a head-butt. Stunned, August staggered back. She cradled her right fist, then tried to spin up into a high kick.

Buffy ducked in, slammed her palm into August's upper chest, and knocked her down. The gash in her side did not slow her, nor did her dislocated shoulder or her broken nose.

"Get up," Buffy told her. "Stop this. If I have to, I'll break both your arms, but I don't want to have to feed you for the next few months."

August glared at her, beyond reason. The crazed girl leaped up again, back into a battle stance, despite her shattered fist.

"Damn you," Buffy whispered.

With a cry of anguish, August launched a blow with her good hand. Buffy dodged, but the girl followed through, stepped into her blow, past Buffy, then brought her arm back and shot an elbow at the back of Buffy's head.

Furious, Buffy stumbled forward and then turned to see August lunging at her again. The steel table was behind her. Buffy hopped up on top of it, avoiding August's attack. Then she kicked out at the girl's damaged hand and August shrieked with pain and staggered back.

Tears sprang to August's face again. She stood for a moment, panting, glaring at Buffy. "They need us, don't you get it?"

"Not like this," Buffy said softly. "Not like this."

"I won't stop," August vowed. "One of us is going to die."

Buffy only shook her head in denial and clutched her dislocated arm against her body.

August rushed the table. Buffy dove into the air, executed a somersault over the girl's head and landed on both feet. In one fluid motion, she shot a hard kick up at the younger Slayer's head. August tried to dodge. She was a scant heartbeat too slow.

There was no time for Buffy to even try to abort the attack. The kick caught the other girl in the side of the neck, just where her jaw met her neck. With a wet snap, her spinal column broke right at the top, and her corpse tumbled backward with the force of the kick and rolled in a heap across the stone floor.

August did not move, not even a twitch. Buffy knew she was dead.

"Oh God, no," Buffy whispered.

Hot tears came into her eyes, but her grief was quickly overcome by anger. "Dammit, no!" she shouted. "No! No! No!"

With her good hand she covered her eyes, spun around in a small circle. It *was* a nightmare. It *had* to be. But the raging pain in her shoulder and the copper taste of her own blood on her lips, was real.

The girl in front of her, August, a Slayer, was dead. That was real.

"How?" she whispered. "It wasn't supposed to be like this. Stupid girl . . ."

But she was not sure if that last part was meant to be addressed to August or to herself. It was cruel, without doubt. All this time alone, then finally contact with not just another human being, but a person who was part of the same mission. And now this.

Her tears felt cold on her cheeks compared to the heat of her blood. Buffy knelt by August and pushed a lock of her hair away from her fine, Italian features, and just studied her for a moment. She wondered if she herself had ever looked so young.

New hatred welled up within her, bearing a razor edge sharper than anything she had felt in years. They had taken Giles from her, Camazotz and his vampire hordes. They had imprisoned her. But they had never been able to take even a sliver of her hope and her faith.

Until now.

Teeth gritted together, a violent surge of adrenaline making Buffy bounce slightly on her feet. She used her good hand to drag August around near the front of the cell, only inches from the door. It would hit her when it opened.

Where August's corpse had lain, she knelt, took a breath, and whacked her broken nose with an open hand. She let the cry of pain come, and sagged a bit. Then she bent over and let blood flow onto the floor. After a couple of minutes, she rolled up the back of her shirt and felt for the puncture wound left in her side by the broken plastic that had impaled her. The wound had already begun to heal.

Buffy used her fingernail to dig it open.

Again, she bled.

But the loss of blood did not weaken her. For it was not her own lifeblood that drove her now, but hatred for her enemy, like nothing she had ever felt before. Her world had been gray for so long that she could remember almost nothing else. Gray and numb and lifeless.

It had color again. The world was crimson as her blood, and black as a vampire's heart.

She allowed herself only one more minute to recover, to breathe slowly. Then she stood and went to the sink, still cradling her dislocated arm. She sat on the floor. With some difficulty, she managed to wrap both hands around the pipe that came down from beneath the sink. Strong hand over the weak one, holding it in place, she planted her feet against the wall under the sink, took a breath, and pushed out as hard as she could.

An awkward angle, but there was enough force behind it to snap the shoulder back into the joint. It felt as though someone were trying to separate the bones with a jagged knife. Buffy could have stopped the scream by biting through her lip. She did not.

Her mouth opened and she shrieked loud and long, releasing all the pain and misery she had been holding inside. Somehow she managed to find her feet and stumbled to the shattered plastic shelving. She snatched up a splintered piece, brought it to her flesh, and sliced a long, clean, horizontal cut across her throat.

Buffy hissed air in through her clenched teeth, for the cut stung, but it was superficial. Nothing vital was hit. After her shoulder, it was almost nothing.

Quivering from the pain and her emotional turmoil, she staggered to the place where she had made herself bleed. A small pool of her blood was there on the stone. Not enough, to her eyes, but it would have to do.

She dropped the plastic dagger to the floor a foot away, then lay down on her side, right cheek already sticky where it touched the edge of the puddle of her blood.

Maddox stormed down the corridor with a cigarette clenched firmly in his lips and a two foot stun-prod gripped in his right hand. One of the guards—a rookie named Theo who was practically a newborn—followed behind him like a puppy.

"Whaddaya think's goin' on, Maddox?" Theo cooed excitedly. "There were screams and everything.

Sounded pretty nasty. Got a serious Slayer catfight, I think. Woulda loved to've seen that."

"We'll see."

They rounded a corner and Maddox saw four other guards up ahead, the two who were supposed to be on the door, and two others who had likely come down from the upper level when the commotion began.

"What the hell's going on?" Maddox demanded.

"Told you, Maddox," Theo said, grinning. "They're tearing each other apart in there. When you said put the new girl in there, that's the last thing I expected."

With a grunt, Maddox froze. He turned to stare at Theo. "Who sired you?"

Theo blinked. "Um, Harmony did."

Maddox sighed. "Of course she did."

Then he tapped Theo's chest lightly with the stun-prod. The vampire jerked and shuddered as electricity surged through him. His eyes were wide, white against the black tattoo Maddox thought he brought shame to. Theo slumped to the ground, jerking a bit. He opened his mouth and a tiny bit of bloody drool spilled out with the tip of his tongue, which he had bitten off.

With a sigh, Maddox turned to the four guards. They were proper vampires, eyes crackling orange, grim-faced, not at all perturbed by what they had seen. Or, at least, not revealing it if they were.

"Remind me to kill Harmony," he said.

The others all nodded, once, silently.

"You're ready?"

Each of them unsnapped a prod similar to the one Maddox held, only smaller and more portable. Maddox could smell the blood inside the room, the scent seeping beneath the steel door. It worried him. He was responsible for what happened within that cell.

Anxious, he gestured to the guards. "Open the door."

The one in front, Brossi, glanced once at Maddox. Other than Maddox, he was the only one who had been there from the beginning. The two of them had been part of the group that had captured Buffy Summers in the first place. They knew what she was capable of.

The door itself was testament to that. There were three locks, equidistant from one another. Each controlled an inch-thick iron deadbolt that, when engaged, locked into a metal casing that itself was plugged into the center of the three-foot-thick stone wall that framed the door. There were two more deadbolts each at the top and bottom of the door, though these had no locks.

It took Brossi a few seconds to unlock the door, then disengage the three main bolts. He hesitated for a moment, turned to glance at Maddox, and then his face changed, forehead erupting into the brutal guise of the vampire. His fangs lengthened and he ran his tongue over them.

Maddox had more control than that, but he did not blame Brossi for feeling threatened. Every time they opened that door, twice a day, they had to be prepared for a fight. Just when they thought Summers was beaten into submission, that was when she was most likely to attack again. When he had been instructed to put the new girl into the same cell, Maddox had balked. It was just asking for trouble. No question it was going to make feeding time even more difficult.

But this was the last thing he had expected.

"Careful," Maddox told the guards.

Brossi slammed back the bolts on the top and bottom of the door, sliding them abruptly out of their metal casings. There was no way to do it quietly, so he opted to do it quickly. The other guards with their stun-prods gathered behind him, tattooed faces expressionless, only the glittering fire of their eyes giving away their anxiety. Maddox stepped up behind them, but at a respectful distance. It was not that he was a coward. Quite the opposite, in fact. If this was some sham and the two Slayers killed them all, it would fall to him to stop them.

"Go!" Maddox ordered.

Brossi shoved the door open with his shoulder, tensed for an attack. The steel door swung eight or nine inches, then hit an obstruction with a dull thump. The vampire guard took a half-step back and prepared to defend himself. Nothing happened, and after a moment, he pushed at the door again, put his weight behind it, and it opened slowly as the obstruction slid out of the way.

"What the hell is that?" Maddox asked, trying to see over the shoulders of the guards.

Half inside the door, Brossi glanced back quickly. "The new girl. She's down."

Cursing loudly, Maddox shoved the others aside and moved up behind Brossi. It was his job not just to keep the Slayers prisoner, but to keep them alive. Maddox peered over Brossi's shoulder, trying to see deeper into the room to make certain Summers wasn't lying in wait. Then he turned and glared at the guards around him.

"Stay back. Either one of them makes it to the door, take her. Break something, burn something, whatever, but I don't have to tell you what will happen if any of you kill one of them."

He gave Brossi a nudge. "Stun her."

Maddox's gaze ticked down to the still form of the teenaged Slayer on the floor, then back at the room. The door was still only partially open, and he could not see Summers anywhere.

She's there, though. A frisson of fear went through him. There was something about the woman that had always given him the creeps a little bit. She was warm and soft, like all humans, and yet there was something almost haunting about her, almost mystical. There was a promise in her eyes every time she looked at him; a promise of payback.

Brossi extended his arm through the open door, stun-prod in hand. Maddox stood back a little, just in case the door should be slammed shut suddenly, his own electrical prod held up at the ready.

As Maddox watched, Brossi tagged the downed Slayer with the prod. Electricity sizzled through her with a crackle and the smell of sizzling hair. The girl did not so much as twitch. There were none of the muscle spasms that electrocution brought.

"Dammit," Maddox whispered. *I'm screwed.*

The girl looked badly beaten. There had been a knock-down, drag-out brawl inside that cell. One Slayer was dead. But what of the other one?

"I'm coming in, Summers. Keep away from the door!" he called into the cell.

Then he motioned Brossi out of the way and kicked the door with all the strength he could muster. Something broke in the corpse on the floor when the door collided with it, but it slid open another half-foot.

Just enough for Maddox to see Buffy Summers lying in a pool of her own blood, bruised and beaten, throat slit, eyes wide and cold and staring right at him.

"No!" Maddox screamed. He struck out at the air, then rammed a fist against the door with a clang and did not even feel the pain. "Dammit, no!"

Furious, and filled with terror as he began to wonder what fate awaited him now, Maddox strode into the room. His stun-prod hung at his side. Astonished, he stared around at the shattered plastic shelving, the clothes strewn about. From a distance, he examined the splintered piece of plastic that had obviously been used to slash Buffy's throat.

"Maddox, how . . .?" Brossi began to ask.

His words trailed off when Maddox glared at him. "New girl cut Summers's throat. Summers broke her neck before she died."

"I don't know," Brossi said slowly. "Better keep back from her. Give her a few volts before you get too close."

Maddox hesitated. Then he studied the Slayer's eyes, the haunting eyes that had promised him death so many times. There was nothing there now. Like tarnished marbles, they were.

The way she lay, mouth partially open, the blood from the wound in her throat had pooled up against her lips. That was the thing that convinced Maddox. That whole side of her face, her hair, her nose, lay in blood, and with her mouth open like that, if she were alive, well . . . she would have been able to taste it. Her own blood. Like a vampire.

Her chest did not move. Her eyes were dead ice fragments. But it was that one detail that convinced him.

Still, Maddox was cautious as he reached out with the stun-prod. The eyes still gave him a chill. The tip of the prod swept toward the woman's eyes, but there wasn't so much as a flinch. Just for safety's sake, he touched the prod against her shoulder. The body jerked slightly, but he'd seen that before. The electricity that surged through the corpse was enough to do that. The hair on the dead woman's head shivered and even floated a bit with the static.

"She's dead," Maddox said, forlorn. "What the hell do I do now?"

He was about to prod her eyes when a thought

occurred to him. Maddox turned and looked at Brossi.

"Or is she?" he said, grinning. "I mean, *he* never comes here, right? We'll just lock it up again, leave them here."

Brossi's expression was grave. "When the new Slayer shows up, he'll know."

"We could be gone by then," Maddox replied sharply. "It's a big world."

Brossi hung his head, all the tension going out of him. In the corridor, the other guards were wide-eyed with the realization of their fate. One of them, Haskell, cut and ran right then, his footsteps echoing back down the corridor. For a moment, Brossi turned in that direction, then regarded Maddox again.

"There isn't anywhere far enough," he said. "It's over, Maddox."

"I never even wanted this job!" Maddox shouted, his voice echoing in the cell.

Mind spinning, he turned back toward Summers again. Rage and fear building inside him, Maddox swung back his leg to kick the corpse. His boot thunked into her flesh . . . *moving* flesh. As if it were part of his own motion, she closed herself around his leg, crawling halfway up it, and snapped it at the knee.

Maddox screamed.

As he went down, he felt the prod tugged from his grasp, and then Buffy Summers, the Slayer, stood over him, her resurrection as sudden as a vampire's, but far more shocking to him.

Despite the pain of his shattered leg, he grinned. She wasn't dead.

"Maddox!" Brossi shouted.

"Don't kill her!" Maddox roared.

The other guards, against his previous orders, began to enter the cell. They all seemed to be moving in slow motion in comparison to the Slayer, and each had a kind of vacant, frightened look in his eyes. He did not blame them. Summers had only ever been a captive to them, but in all that time, they had never underestimated how dangerous she was.

Once upon a time, Camazotz had kept the existence of the Slayer hidden from his Kakchiquels, but that had changed after her capture. They had all heard tales of the Slayers now, and knew that Summers was among the most dangerous who had ever lived. For their entire community, the girl locked in this custom dungeon had become almost mythical.

Now they had seen her dead. She had taken a hit from the prod and barely reacted. She had lost a great deal of blood. It was almost as though what they fought was a horrible specter of the Slayer, rather than mere flesh and blood. Not a woman, but a bogeyman so terrible even the creatures of darkness feared her.

They had barely kept her caged all this time.

And now she had a weapon.

In the dim light of the stone room, Maddox

reached out for the metal table and struggled to rise. The Slayer moved so fast he could barely keep his eyes on her. All in all, it would have been much better if she had had a stake. Brossi was electrocuted and then decapitated. The other two were disarmed before she broke them. Maddox could only watch.

Then she came for him.

CHAPTER 2

Exhilaration shot through Buffy as she rushed down the corridor toward a red, glowing EXIT sign. The sign itself—an indication that this place had originally been used by humans—made the whole scene almost surreal, and she felt giddy with her freedom.

Freedom.

But she wasn't free yet. Her captors had kept a hood over her head when they brought her here years before, so she had no idea what surrounded the building she was in. Things were bad. That was all she had learned from August, but it was enough to set her nerves on edge.

Thoughts of August made her flinch and swallow hard. Nausea roiled in her gut and bile rose up in the back of her throat. The girl had forced her hand, and even then Buffy had done everything she could to avoid killing her, but August was dead. When she thought of that, and the things she'd had to do to herself to feign her own death, her feet began to slow beneath her.

Buffy could not afford to slow down.

She took a deep breath, picked up her pace again, and silently cursed the vampires for not having any wood around. A chair leg, anything at all, would have made it possible for her to dust them without feeling so much like it had been a massacre.

In her mind, she saw a quick flash of herself slamming the huge steel door closed on Maddox's neck, severing his head. The spray of dust that had resulted was welcome, but despite her years of hatred for her jailer, there was no triumph in it.

Not that she had any sympathy, either. What unnerved her was that the deaths she had dealt out to the guards had been so intimate. She did not want to get that close to the undead. Not ever. They were abominations, unclean things; a truth she had come to realize more and more during her captivity. Her calling was to eliminate them, but it was a filthy job.

The sick feeling in her stomach abated somewhat, but a faint, sour taste remained in her mouth. She shook her head once to clear her mind, then shoved through the door at the end of the hall. It swung too wide, and would have clanged off the wall if she had not caught it quickly enough.

A momentary pause to be certain no one was near,

and then she started up a set of stairs in front of her. A long oak railing was bolted to the wall. Buffy stopped halfway up and lashed out with a snap kick that cracked the railing in two. The halves dangled down, tearing at their moorings. Another kick, aimed at one of the sagging halves, and a fifteen-inch length of splintered oak clattered to the stairs. The Slayer snatched it and continued upward.

It was too thick by far. Her grip did not come close to reaching all the way around it. But it would do. It would most certainly do.

There was a door at the top of the stairs. As she raced toward it, the door began to open. A vampire poked his head into the stairwell with a predator's curiosity, his nostrils flaring as he scented the air. The black tattoo splayed across his features, bat wings extending down his cheeks into a thin beard, made the blazing orange fire of his eyes stand out in ghostly fashion, there in the darkened stairwell.

Those ghostfire eyes widened as he spotted her. "Oh, sh—"

Buffy pivoted and popped a kick at the door. It clanged into his head and the vampire stumbled back into the corridor. She hauled the door open and pursued him.

Though she sensed some alarm in him, the vampire faced her without hesitation. "She's out!" he yelled into the empty corridor. "The Slayer's out!"

"Tattletale," Buffy rasped.

Expressionless, she backhanded him. He tried to

block the blow, but she was too fast for him. Faster than ever before. It had been a long time since she had fought anything but shadows, and it was going to take some getting used to, but she was at almost her most powerful now.

The makeshift oak stake flashed down and punched an enormous hole in his chest. The vampire dusted.

From around a corner off to her left came the sound of running feet. Her eyes flickered closed for a moment: three, no four of them. Though the stake felt good in her hand, and though she wanted to eliminate all of her captors, her priorities began to assert themselves.

Primary among them was simply to get out, to escape, to see the sky again. To breathe fresh air.

Buffy took off down the corridor, away from her pursuers. The structure she was in appeared to have once housed offices, for there were doors and glass windows looking inward all along the hall. Each office was dark and lifeless inside. The hallway itself had no external windows, however. At least not here.

Up ahead, the hall turned right. Buffy rounded the corner just as she heard shouts behind her. The vampires had seen her. That was all right, though. She could practically smell the outdoors now. Nothing was going to stand in her way.

Even as that thought skittered across her brain, she looked up. At the end of the hall in front of her, the structure opened up into a wide lobby area. The door was all glass. The walls on either side of the door were glass. All of it was painted black.

A pair of vampires stood blocking the door, arms crossed. They did not flinch as she approached, did not even attempt the arrogant, menacing grin that their kind had mastered long ago. But Buffy remembered all too well how this breed of vampires worked, these servants of Camazotz. The demon-god who was their master had trained them to be silent and fearless. Yet she had seen fear in the tattooed eyes of the ones she had killed in her cell, and knew that it was there in them.

"You can get away from the door, or you can *be* the door," she told them grimly.

In unison, they unfolded their arms and prepared to fight her. Behind her, Buffy heard more shouts as her pursuers caught sight of her again. Ahead, the door sentries stood firm, eyes crackling with energy.

Buffy rushed headlong at them without breaking stride. She was three feet away when they lunged for her. The Slayer froze in place, both of the sentries' reach fell short. Buffy leaped up, spun into a roundhouse kick that caught one of the sentries in the jaw and sent him reeling back toward the blacked out glass door.

In the instant before the glass shattered, she punched the splintered oak railing through the heart of the other. As he dusted, his partner crashed through the glass door. The darkness fell away, and the daylight poured in.

The sun.

A grin slipped across Buffy's features as she watched the other sentry scramble to his feet among shards of black glass and try to get inside. He began to smoke, and then to burn, and just before he would have reached the shade, he exploded into a cloud of cinder and ash.

The Slayer stepped calmly out into the sunshine, sneakers crunching shattered glass. Then she turned, bathed in the light, and eyed the bat-faced vampires who had been rushing at her from within. They all stopped short ten feet from the door, avoiding the perilous splash of sun that spread across the floor.

Once upon a time, Buffy would have teased them, said something funny. She didn't feel funny anymore. With a flourish, she made an obscene gesture, turned, and walked away.

But she felt their burning eyes upon her back.

The building she had been in was a three-story office with no name or insignia on the front, and no sign. Only a street number, One Five Seven.

It was a beautiful Southern California day, the kind of glorious day she had always taken for granted growing up. This was, after all, what California was all about. Today, however, she reveled in it. Birds sang. A sparrow glided across the street in front of her. The breeze carried sweet smells to her, like springtime, though she was not sure of the season.

Free.

Though Buffy knew she had to act immediately, to figure out the lay of the land, to find her friends and discover what horror had driven August so wild, she was overwhelmed for several moments simply with being outside again. She had to shield her eyes or look down at the ground for the first few minutes, so unaccustomed was she to the brilliance of the daylight.

A relief surged through her unlike anything she had ever felt. Along with it came a feeling of power, as though some long dead battery within her was being recharged.

The block she was on was lined with faceless buildings similar to the one she had escaped from. Boring corporate shells. As she strode toward an intersection ahead, though, she frowned. Something was not right. Even out here, something was intensely not right.

Disconnected as she had been for so long, it took her a moment to put it together. An ominous feeling descended upon her. Then she knew. It was not the presence of something dreadful, but an absence. The absence of life, of bustle, even of traffic. The birds were the only activity in sight.

Greatly troubled, she began to run again. At the intersection, she glanced both ways along a street dotted with trendy storefront boutiques and sandwich shops. Though she had not been there since shortly after moving to Sunnydale, Buffy recognized the town. She was in El Suerte, maybe fifteen minutes from home.

Hope rose again within her, punctuated by the appearance, far down the street, of several cars crossing at another intersection. Then, off to her left, an engine caught her attention. She turned to see an SUV cruising along among the shops. It halted abruptly in front of a sandwich shop and the driver, a middle-aged man in a well-tailored suit, popped out and took a look around. He spotted her, frowned, then hurried into the shop.

Moments later he emerged again, carrying several plastic bags she presumed were filled with sandwiches and drinks. Buffy's only thought was of home, of getting back to Sunnydale. Quickly, she trotted across the street to catch the man before he could drive away.

"Hey!" she called.

Eyes wide, he stared at her in alarm. Buffy slowed, wondering if he was some sort of paranoid.

"Why aren't you working?" he demanded, gaze darting up and down the street as though afraid he might be seen speaking to someone slacking off.

"Umm, day off?" Buffy shrugged. "Do you know where I can catch a bus to Sunnydale?"

He laughed, but it was a tiny sound, almost as though he were coughing instead. "What are you, some kind of nut? Who in their right mind would ever *want* to go there?"

Again he glanced around. "You better get off the street, sweetheart."

Then he ducked into the SUV and locked the doors even before starting the engine, as though afraid she might try to carjack him. A moment later, he pulled away. Buffy called after him, but he didn't even look into the rearview mirror.

Angry now, she turned toward the sandwich shop, determined to get answers. When she glanced at the door, however, she saw a dark-haired man with a thick mustache turning a key in the lock. He pulled back from the door when their eyes met, as if he did not want to be seen. Then he closed the blinds that hung by the door, and she could not see him or the inside of the shop anymore.

"What the hell's wrong with you people?" Buffy shouted.

But a deep dread had filled her, a horrible feeling that she knew exactly what was wrong with them. It was impossible, of course. A whole town could not be terrorized like this. But they were.

A sudden squeal from a siren startled her. Buffy turned to see a police car cruising slowly toward her. It rolled up beside her. Two cops jumped out with the engine still running and began to walk toward her. They began to reach for their weapons.

"Excuse me, Miss Summers, but we're going to have to ask you to come with us."

Miss Summers. They knew who she was. They were looking for her. Her suspicion of moments earlier had become a reality. The people terrified to be on the streets, the police looking for her. She had not been the only captive in El Suerte. The vampires held the entire town prisoner.

The two police officers drew their weapons and aimed at her.

"Miss Summers."

"I don't think so," Buffy replied. "It isn't as though they're going to let you kill me."

One of the cops, a tall, dark-complexioned guy with sad eyes, looked extremely uncomfortable. His partner was a heavyset man with pasty skin and thick glasses.

Pastyface smiled. "I can shoot both kneecaps, maybe your shoulders. You'll recover, but it'll hurt like hell. One way or another, you're coming with us."

Buffy sighed. "I don't think so. Thanks for the ride, though."

Pastyface looked confused. With a single, fluid motion, Buffy spiraled in the air toward him and kicked the gun from his hand, shattering his fingers in the process. He let out a scream even as the tall man fired. Buffy was still in motion, however, and the bullet whistled past her cheek, close enough that she could feel the air pressure change by her skin.

Then the tall man stared down at his hand, stunned that his gun had somehow disappeared. Buffy showed it to him, then tossed it over her shoulder. As he watched it sail through the air, she punched him hard enough to spin him around. He tumbled like a felled redwood on top of his partner.

Alarm bells continued to go off in her head, but they had nothing to do with the cops. They were practically forgotten already. All she could think of was the reaction of the sandwich man in the SUV when she had mentioned Sunnydale.

Who in their right mind would ever want to go there?

He lived in El Suerte, a prisoner of the vampires who ran the town, and he thought the idea of anyone going to Sunnydale was crazy.

Tendrils of ice spread throughout her body, wrapping around her spine and curling up in her gut. Grim-faced, she went to the police car and slid into the driver's seat. As she put it in gear she caught sight of her reflection in the rearview mirror.

A shock ran through her.

For just a moment, she saw herself at nineteen. Then the illusion faded and she saw the way she truly looked, the hard line of her jaw, the ragged cut of her long, blond hair, the crinkles at the corners of her eyes and mouth, the furious glare of her eyes. It was startling, after so long, to see her own reflection. She saw that it was not only the world they had changed, but her as well.

Buffy hated them all the more for it.

In her mind, she saw again the image of herself at nineteen. That was how it was supposed to be. None of this was meant to happen. For a short while, she had almost forgotten that. Yet again the voice of her younger self rose up within her, took control.

I've got to get back. I've got to fix this.

The words meant so many things. Whatever was happening in the here and now, she had to do something about it, true. But that was the older Buffy's priority. Within her body was also a girl out of time, a college girl who only ever wanted to be normal. A young woman who had been told by a ghost that she would make a mistake that would have catastrophic results. She could not help but think that she lived amongst those results even now.

I have to go back, she thought again. *Figure out what I did wrong, find a way back, and stop it.* It never occurred to her to wonder if such a thing were possible. After all, the being called The Prophet had somehow cast the spirit of her younger self forward to inhabit her future body. If that was possible, there had to be a way to reverse the process.

For the moment, though, she had to figure out just how far the vampires' influence had spread, and stop them. It was what she did, who she was. The Slayer. Before The Prophet had touched her, had sent her forward in time, Buffy had been determined to dedicate herself wholly to being the Slayer, and also to having a life of her own. One hundred percent Slayer, one hundred percent Buffy. An impossible task, but she had done impossible things before. Yet that struggle had frustrated those close to her, and might have indirectly led to her current situation. If she had not made such a mess of things, she would never have been in a position to rely upon The Prophet, would never have ended up here.

A grim smile cut through her melancholy now. For in this future she did not have to worry about trying to live two lives to their fullest, about filling two roles. The things that had made up the life of Buffy Summers seemed to have been torn away, leaving only this monstrous landscape where vampires ruled. No one needed Buffy anymore. She didn't need to live two lives . . . only one.

She was just the Slayer now. There was a freedom in that, and it felt good.

Knuckles white where she gripped the steering wheel, she accelerated and raced out of El Suerte, headed for Sunnydale. Soon enough, they would know she had taken the car. Her only hope was that they would not realize where she was headed.

Though she tried not to, Buffy wondered what had become of her mother and her friends, her old gang. Not only now, but *then*. Willow, Oz, Xander, and Anya. Not to mention Giles, and even Angel. What had happened to them that day, after The Prophet had cast her out of her body?

In the past . . .

It was difficult to breathe. Willow glanced around the dorm room she shared with Buffy, and shuddered. It was a pretty big room, but she felt claustrophobic in it for the first time. Oz sat beside her, and she reached out to squeeze his hand for reassurance. Xander and Anya were there as well. Quite a crowd for her little summoning, in the darkened room, with the shades pulled down.

But even in the darkness, the thing that shimmered in the middle of the room, beside Buffy, was darker still. It made her think of black holes, the way it swirled, oily and black, there in the air, a rip in the fabric of the world.

Willow had summoned Lucy Hanover, the ghost of a long-dead Slayer, who now aided lost souls in the afterworld. The ghost had heard dire predictions from this thing, called The Prophet, and had agreed to try to bring it forth to communicate those prophecies more precisely.

But now that it was here, Willow only wanted to send the thing back. Just being in its presence made her skin crawl like nothing she had ever felt before. And now it seemed to float nearer to Buffy; or, perhaps more accurately, it seemed to consume the space between them, to slither across reality as it reached for her.

No! Willow thought. *Buffy, don't let it near!* But somehow she had lost the strength to cry out.

The specter of Lucy Hanover lingered, hovering near the window, watching the proceedings as Buffy spoke to The Prophet. The entity's words stunned them all.

"The future cannot be prevented now. Already the clockwork grinds on," it said, voice like whispered profanity. *"But I can show you my vision, share with you the sight, so you may see what is coming and perhaps better prepare for it."*

Buffy flinched away from it and glanced over at Willow. Silently, she urged the Slayer to say no. Anxiously, Willow bit her lip. The ghost of Lucy Hanover reached out phantom hands toward Buffy as though she wanted to help. But she was already dead. This was all the help she could offer.

Buffy sat up straighter and stared at The Prophet, the flowing black presence in the room. "Show me."

Willow shook her head slowly, warning, but Buffy did not see. Still, somehow, she felt unable to speak.

"I must only touch you, and you may see."

"Do it," Buffy instructed The Prophet.

The Prophet's slick, shimmering form slithered toward her. The tear in the fabric of the world extended toward her, fingers like tendrils reached for her.

Finally, Willow felt something give way within her, as though the grip of some hideous force had finally loosened.

"Buffy," she said cautiously. "Maybe this isn't such a good—"

But it was too late. The Prophet touched Buffy. And Buffy screamed.

The Slayer's eyes went wide and she stared as though she were seeing a vision of unspeakable horror. Her mouth remained open but the ragged, high-pitched scream died on her lips. Her chest began to heave, and Buffy started to hyperventilate.

"Buffy!" Willow cried.

She ran to her best friend and grabbed hold just as Buffy began to fall limp. Angry, and fearful for her, Willow glanced around the room. Oz was beside her, Xander and Anya behind him, looking on worriedly.

Otherwise the room was empty.

"Where . . . where'd they go?" Willow asked softly.

The others glanced around as well, apparently equally mystified.

"That's just like a disembodied clairvoyant," Xander muttered. "Offer up the ominous future, then skip town before the questions start rolling in."

"I'm going to open the shade now. I've had enough darkness for today," Anya said in clipped tones.

When the shades were up, and the sunlight streamed in, Willow felt a little better. Buffy was still breathing, though her eyes were closed and she was pale. Her skin felt too cold.

But she was alive. And she was the Slayer.

"What do you think's up?" Oz asked.

Willow swallowed hard. "Well, I'm sorta hoping I'm wrong. And it bothers me to think about how often I feel that way. But I'm guessing whatever future that thing showed Buffy, it was too much for her to handle. Kinda think she's in shock."

"Whoa. Red light," Xander said. "She's the Slayer. How could just seeing something put her into a state of shock?"

"I'm thinkin' it depends what she saw," Oz noted.

Anya threw her hands up in exasperation. "See! Why does this stuff always happen?" She rounded on Xander, a small pout on her lips. "Why do we live *here?* In all the world, *this* is where you want to live? Can't we go far away from the impending apocalypse?"

"You could," Willow said sadly, still gazing at her

best friend's pale features. "But that wouldn't keep it from coming."

For another few moments, Willow cradled Buffy gently in her arms. Then, with a suddenness that gave her a start, the Slayer opened her eyes. Her skin was still cold and white, but her eyes were as fierce and determined as always.

Fierce and determined . . . and yet there was something else there as well.

"Buffy!" Willow cried.

"See!" Xander said. "She's okay."

Buffy sat up and shook Willow's hands off her. She stretched like a cat, as if testing her body to see if she was harmed in some way. Flexing her fingers, she stared at her hands as though they were some newly invented marvel. Then she stood up carefully, a bit off-balance. She nearly collapsed, and Willow thought of a foal just testing its legs for the first time.

"You are okay, right?" Xander asked doubtfully.

The Slayer glanced around the dorm room. A sly grin stole across her features for one moment, and then was gone. She went to the closet, reached inside and grabbed a black leather jacket, though it was too warm outside for the coat.

"Buffy?" Willow asked. "Come on. I know you want to protect us, but we're part of this. It's our future, too. What did you see?"

As she slipped the jacket on, Buffy turned to regard them all. There was no emotion on her face now.

Her eyes flickered with some sort of light, as though from within.

"Everything will be fine," she said, a peculiar slurring to her voice.

"You're not all right," Willow told her. "Come on. Just give yourself an hour's rest. Then we'll figure out what to do about Giles. You've got to talk to us, Buffy. Let us help."

But Buffy shook her head. "There is nothing you can do."

"So you're going to go after Giles alone, after all this?" Xander demanded.

He sounded ticked off, and Willow didn't blame him.

"Do not concern yourself," Buffy said bluntly.

With that, the Slayer turned and left the room, not even bothering to close the door behind her.

"Great," Xander sighed. "Now she's back to that again. Omnipotent Slayer-girl. Taking it all on herself."

"I don't know," Willow said slowly, staring at the half-open door.

Oz sidled up beside her. "What don't you know?" he asked, brow furrowed.

"I don't think this is about that," she said. "This is something else. Something new and family-size creepy. Or, okay, could be just Willow-paranoia. But I'm thinking The Prophet touching Buffy? Possibly more to it than just a Viewmaster of Doom."

"There was a sinister vibe around that thing," Anya agreed. "But what do you think it did, exactly?"

Willow stared at the door. "Remember the part where I said 'I don't know?' "

"Well, we'll keep an eye on her. See what's what," Xander suggested.

Willow nodded, deeply troubled, and afraid for Buffy. She didn't know if the future was going to be as The Prophet had predicted, but she had a sinking feeling it was going to be ugly, one way or another.

As she drove along nearly deserted roads, Buffy was chilled by the changes she saw around her. A few cars passed by, and some stores were open, but many others were boarded up. The skating rink just off I-17 had been partially destroyed by fire, and the parking lot was cracked and overgrown. There were no rollerbladers, no joggers, no bicyclists. Other than those few cars, the only people she saw were a pair of homeless men raiding a Dumpster behind a Chinese restaurant that was apparently still in operation, and they scrambled back through a broken fence behind the place when she drove by.

Buffy decided it was perhaps best to enter the town quietly, perhaps even invisibly. They'd be looking for the car, after all. Buffy ditched the El Suerte police car in the overgrown lot that had once been the Sunnydale Twin Drive-In.

It rolled across the cracked pavement, four-foot weeds whisking against the grille of the car. Buffy killed the engine, took a long breath, and laid her forehead upon the steering wheel for a moment. A slight motion, and she flinched at the sudden pain in her broken nose. Along with her other wounds, it had begun to heal quickly. That was part of being the Slayer. But it was still very sore.

Resolute, she popped open the door and climbed out, then hesitated. Inside the police car was a shotgun locked in a brace between seats. It would be a simple thing to snap the brace and take it with her. Buffy glanced into the car and looked at the gleaming barrel of the gun. Then she shook her head. What she wanted was a crossbow. Maybe even a sword. But after all this time she suspected that the weapons caches at Giles's apartment and her mother's house, not to mention her dorm room back at U.C. Sunnydale, would have been cleaned out. Even if they were still there, the Kakchiquels, Camazotz's vampire followers, would likely be keeping an eye on those places in case she should return.

Without those weapons, without even a knife, she would have to fashion some crude, makeshift stakes, and hope that was enough.

Buffy left the car where it was and began to walk back toward the road. After a moment she paused and glanced back at the concrete structure on the far side of the lot that had once served as both projection booth and concession stand. Once upon a time, like any abandoned structure in Sunnydale, it had been a prime nesting place for vampires and other creatures of darkness.

Best to make sure, she thought.

In a light jog, she crossed the lot without any attempt to hide herself. If anyone were inside the bunker-like edifice, they would already have seen her. The metal door was rusted and hung off its hinges. The sky above was blue as a robin's egg, the wind whispered through the overgrown brush in the lot, the sunlight painted the world around her in bright hues. But the beauty of the day ended at that rusty door. The gaping maw of the place almost seemed to swallow the sunlight. Within was impenetrable darkness.

Nothing moved inside.

Buffy kicked the door loose and it crashed down onto concrete inside. She paused for a moment, then slipped into the dark. It took a moment for her eyes to adjust. Blinking, she ventured farther into the now gray, dusty interior of the building.

Nothing. Something scuffled in the walls, but that was all. It was little more than a tomb for several generations of mice. There were counters of shattered glass where concession snacks had once been offered. Empty now.

Head cocked to one side, Buffy listened, searching for some sound that did not represent rodents. Convinced she was alone, she turned to leave and then thought better of it. Upstairs in the projection booth she was likely to find furniture of some kind. And it was easier to turn smashed furniture into stakes than to forge them out of downed tree limbs, particularly when she had nothing to whittle with.

Sure enough, at the top of the stairs, in the box of a

room where the projectionist had once done his work, she found a small table and several wooden chairs, the legs of which would be satisfactory for her purposes. Buffy crossed to the table, pulled out the nearest chair, and froze with astonishment as she gazed at what lay upon it.

A crossbow.

More accurately, *her* crossbow, the one Giles had given her when they first began to train together. Beside it, a folded bone-white card with two words printed neatly on the front: FOR BUFFY.

Doubt flooded her and she glanced around anxiously, suddenly sure she must have been mistaken. Someone had to be here—otherwise how could she explain the weapon's presence?

Yet her senses confirmed it. She was alone.

Tentatively, she reached out to pick up the crossbow, studying it intently to be sure there was no tripwire or other trap involved. There was not. Only the crossbow, and on the chair opposite that one, a small quiver containing bolts for it.

Profoundly unnerved, a thousand questions in her head, Buffy shattered one of the chairs, snapped the legs and back into half a dozen usable stakes, and carried them under one arm with the quiver. In the other hand she held the crossbow. On alert, skin prickling as she searched around her for any sign of another presence, she hurried down the stairs and out into the sun.

With the blue sky above, she felt a little better, but

not much. This was a mystery that disturbed her deeply. Someone had known or at least suspected that she would find her way to this spot, or had been here upon her arrival and left these things for her to find.

And all across the lot, the shadows cast by nearby trees and the remnants of the drive-in screens had grown longer. The afternoon was waning, and night was only a few hours away.

Buffy hurried to the police car again. She opened the trunk, and was relieved to find a canvas bag that had belonged to one of the police officers inside. There were cotton sweatpants and a sweatshirt in there, as well as a large pair of sneakers. She dumped the clothes out, dropped the weapons into the bag, then noticed a small box of roadside flares and took those as well. She slung the bag over her shoulder and headed, not for the road, but for the chain link fence at the far side of the lot.

It felt to her as though there were eyes upon her, now. The crossbow was almost warm in her grip. Buffy vaulted the fence and set off through a stretch of woods that would lead up to a power plant, from which she could work her way eventually into Hammersmith Park, and then into the backyards of residential Sunnydale.

Stay off the street, she told herself.

CHAPTER 3

If the silence in El Suerte had been surreal, the ravaged streets of Sunnydale were all *too* real. As Buffy made her way through back alleys and across fire escapes, hugging the shadows to keep out of plain sight, a constant current of alarm and abhorrence ran through her body. Her town had become an abomination.

The parks were ravaged, statues destroyed. Every few blocks she passed a row of buildings or houses that had been burned out completely, leaving a charred shell behind. It was unnerving, seeing some shops and markets apparently thriving, while so many other businesses had been ransacked, shattered windows in the front a sure sign of what she would find inside.

Three times she had entered such a store, and each time the result was the same. Christabel's Consignments, The Flower Cart, and Quarryhouse Pizza. Each store had been torn apart, ripped and shattered, but it had obviously happened long ago and a thick layer of dust, umblemished by the footprint of a single intruder, lay upon everything. In the back of each of those businesses, Buffy discovered the remains of the owners, so decayed that there was no way to tell how they died. She could only assume the vampires had killed them.

And yet the others, the stores that were still running, were equally disturbing to see, for Buffy knew that their proprietors must be cooperating with the vampires, serving both the humans who still lived in Sunnydale and the monsters who ruled it.

With each block she drove, Buffy's mood became even more grim. Questions about her mother's fate, and that of her friends, kept forcing their way into her mind, but Buffy pushed them away. Before she could help anyone, she had to know exactly what the situation was, what she was dealing with. Someone had been there, at the Twin Drive-In. They knew she was on her way here. No way could she risk going by her house just yet.

In a way, despite her horror at the devastation that had occurred in some places in town, it disturbed her even more deeply when she saw that other businesses and homes seemed remarkably well-preserved. Downtown was deserted, and yet many of the businesses actually still had lights on. Curious, Buffy broke in through the back door of the Espresso Pump. The machines hummed quietly, the coolers still working, red lights winking on coffee machines, ready for business.

Buffy made her way through the darkened store to the front door and looked at the posted hours of business. There were three words printed there: OPEN ALL NIGHT. Simple enough, but they created more questions. The Espresso Pump was still in operation, as were most of the bars she had seen, as well as video stores, a couple of small markets, and the Sun Cinema. But were they run by vampires or humans? *Were* there many humans left?

As she had made her way around town, she had seen several police cars cruising slowly down deserted streets. *Probably looking for me,* she'd thought. But she had also seen a few other vehicles, including two gray vans with no rear windows and blacked-out windshields.

Just inside the Espresso Pump, Buffy stepped back a bit from the door when she saw another of those gray vans cruise by slowly. It seemed too quiet, almost as though it were rolling along without an engine. Ridiculous, of course. She had not heard anything because of the hum of the many machines inside the café. But eerie nevertheless.

A car pulled up in front of the Sun Cinema across the street. Buffy was only slightly surprised to see a haggard-looking middle-aged couple climb out together. They walked around to the trunk, from which they retrieved a trio of large film canisters. Revulsion rippled through her as she realized what was going on. These people were collaborators. Whatever was in the canisters, they were films that had been brought in to be screened for the vampires that now populated Sunnydale.

Maybe they had no choice, Buffy thought. But she knew that they all had a choice, the people who still lived in this town. Some of them might not be cooperating with the vampires, but rather were paralyzed by their fear, too terrified to fight. The people remaining in Sunnydale could have banded together and killed their masters, or simply run off while the sun was up. Some probably *had* fled. But Buffy knew that she would have to be careful. Whether collaborators or simply ruled by their fear, she could not afford to trust anyone who was still here.

The whole town belonged to the monsters now, one enormous lair for the vampires she had come to know as Kakchiquels, the servants of Camazotz. With this as the epicenter, they were building a kingdom, an empire even. Their control extended at least to El Suerte, probably farther.

Buffy needed answers.

As soon as the human couple had disappeared inside the theater, Buffy went back out into the alley behind the Espresso Pump again. With the canvas bag of weapons slung across her back, she moved lithely through the hidden places of Sunnydale, always alert for watchful eyes. Even the humans here could not be trusted, that much was now certain.

The going was slow due to the need for stealth, but within twenty minutes she found herself on a block of warehouses, factories and office buildings that ran parallel to the street where the Bronze sat. There were other bars there as well, and it stood to reason she might be able to catch a human out during the daylight.

Answers. The need to hear it from the lips of a living, breathing human being was strong in here. Her instinct, and her own memories of the place, had suggested this would be a good neighborhood to start. If that didn't work, she might try at the college, or simply break into a home that looked as though it were still occupied.

It had occurred to her that the initial skirmishes she'd had with the Kakchiquels all those years ago had been in Docktown, but it would take too long for her to get over there. She had a couple of hours, probably less, before dark. If possible, she wanted to be out of Sunnydale by then. Otherwise she would need a safe place to use as her base, and had no idea where to begin.

Buffy slid between an enormous trash bin and the brick wall of a warehouse. Fifteen feet above the ground was an iron ladder that led to the roof. Without hesitation, she splayed her hands against the brick on one side and the metal bin on the other and crawled up between the two. Muscles rippled like cables in her arms.

With a push off the wall, she landed atop the trash bin, balanced on the metal lip of the thing. Buffy sprang from her perch and both hands locked around the bottom rung of the ladder. Feet against the building, she pulled herself up and then was scrambling hand over hand to the roof.

Crouched low, she sprinted across the rooftop to the opposite corner, where she could see the street that ran in front of the Bronze, as well as the alley beside the building she was on. Disappointment deflated her. The street below was empty of movement of any kind. A stray beer bottle, pushed by the wind, rolled across pavement with a tinkle of glass. Otherwise, all was silence.

For ten minutes or more, Buffy sat there at the edge of the roof. From that height, she could see almost as far as Docktown to the east, the blazing sun on top of the cinema downtown off to the north, and to the south, the tops of houses in residential neighborhoods.

It was as though the entire town had been killed, drained by a vampire. Yet it seethed with menace, as if at any moment its eyes would open, burning orange, and it would rise with fangs gnashing, thirsting for blood.

Anxious, Buffy bounced on the balls of her feet and glanced time and again at the deepening hues of blue on the horizon and the long afternoon shadows on the street.

"I've gotta get out of here," she whispered.

Almost as if on cue, the sound of a distant engine came to her. Buffy crouched down even farther and glanced furtively up and down the street. A moment later, she saw the same gray van—or another exactly like it—cruising toward her.

With a small squeak of brakes, it stopped in front of the Bronze. There was a moment's pause and then the horn blared twice and the passenger door opened.

The figure that emerged from the van made Buffy shiver, though the sun shone warmly on her. She could not see if it was male or female, but it was clothed in a silver radiation suit that covered it from head to toe. Only the black goggles across its eyes broke up the endless silver. Not an inch of skin was visible.

Vampire, she thought, and instantly knew it was true. Daylight reflected off the folds in its silver suit, but the monster was safe within that protective garb.

The driver of the van beeped again and the front door of the Bronze slammed open. A tall human man with black hair came out of the club, hands in the air.

"All right, all right! Keep your shirt on!" he snapped.

The vampire walked around to the back of the van and opened the door. From what Buffy could tell from that angle, there was nothing inside the van. Then the man turned back toward the Bronze and shouted inside.

"Move it! Come on, kiddies. Everyone has to take a turn."

Almost immediately, six more people came out of the club, all in their late teens, early twenties. Three male, three female. One of the girls began to sob and hesitate, unwilling to climb into the van with the others. The dark-haired man went to her, held her face in his hands and whispered something that made her stiffen, wide-eyed. After that she went meekly to the back of the van and climbed in.

The vampire returned to the front of the van, climbed in, and then the vehicle rolled away.

For a moment, the dark-haired man stared after it. Then he went to the door of the Bronze and locked it up before walking to a brand-new convertible Mercedes parked along the road amongst several other cars.

He got in and started the engine. Then he took a moment to tilt his head back and regard himself in the mirror, fussing with his hair.

Which was when Buffy recognized him.

"Oh my God," she whispered. *"Parker."*

The last time she had seen him he had been a freshman in college. He had seduced her, used her, and then pretended he had done nothing wrong. Now he was five years older, and Parker Abrams was not only collaborating with the vampires, he seemed to be enjoying himself.

"Son of a bitch," Buffy muttered angrily.

She withdrew from the edge of the building eight or ten feet, paused, then ran full tilt. With a grunt of effort and anger, she sprang out across the narrow alleyway below. The gap was broader than she had judged and she extended her body forward, turned her leap into a dive. Buffy made it across with room to spare, hit the roof of the Bronze and tucked into a roll.

Without a pause, she flowed back to her feet and ran across the building to stare down at Parker's car. The Mercedes slid into reverse, but moved only two feet as he attempted to pull out from between two other vehicles.

He was right below her.

Buffy leaped out into open air, her hair whipping behind her as she fell straight down, canvas bag dragging behind her like an unopened parachute. Though it lasted only a heartbeat or two, the fall seemed extremely slow to her. Parker had turned the steering wheel and put the car in drive again, and even as she fell he began to pull forward slowly, at pains to be sure he cleared the bumper of the car in front of him.

Her boots slammed the hood of the Mercedes with a loud crumpling noise. The impact made her teeth clack together and drove her to her knees.

Parker screamed in surprise and fear and for just a moment, forgot he was driving. The bumper of the Mercedes rapped lightly against the car in front of it.

He didn't even notice. He only stared at her. "What—" he muttered. "Who the—" Parker's eyes went wide, and she knew then that he had recognized her.

"Oh Jesus. *You.*"

Buffy rose from the dented hood and gripped the top of the convertible's windshield. Parker gripped the wheel, cut it as far to the left as he could, and pressed the accelerator. He clipped the other car's bumper again, but Buffy flipped herself over the windshield and into the passenger's seat.

"No!" Parker yelled.

Beside him now, Buffy shot her right hand out and latched on to his throat, squeezing.

"Stop the car."

Parker slammed on the brakes. "Buffy, please," he rasped hoarsely, eyes roving desperately, searching the streets.

It turned her stomach to think that he might be hoping the vampires might still be there, might protect him from her.

"You remember me. You know who I am. Let me ask you, do you know *what* I am?"

Choking, he managed a wheezing "yes." His eyes were on her, and Buffy stared back at him until Parker looked away. She released his throat and he began to massage it, almost whimpering. When she reached around to pull her canvas bag into her lap, he flinched.

"I'm going to ask questions. You're going to drive. If I think you're lying, I'll snap your neck. Any doubt in your mind that I mean what I say?" she demanded.

He hesitated. Then he smiled, as if relieved. His eyes still had the sparkle that had charmed her once upon a time. "Buffy," he said amiably. "You don't have to threaten me."

Nostrils flaring, she turned to glare at him. "You took advantage of me once, Parker. But that was a long time ago. Do I look like that girl to you now?"

Cowed, he gave her the once-over, then shook his head.

"I'll break you," she promised. "Just drive."

"Where to?"

Her thoughts skittered off in several directions at once. There was no way to know how far Camazotz's influence had spread. But she was certain that there was no way a city the size of Los Angeles could have been overrun. If it had, they wouldn't still be based here in Sunnydale.

"South," she said.

Parker drove.

A car passed going the other direction. She watched to be sure Parker made no attempt to signal the driver, likely another collaborator on his way to open up some business that would serve the vampires. The shadows had grown longer. The sky on the western horizon had begun to darken.

Nightfall was imminent.

"Faster," Buffy instructed.

"Your wish is my command."

"Guess you're pretty good at that response," Buffy snarled. "How long have they been in control here?"

"In Sunnydale? Going on four years, I guess. It started small at first, a few people here and there disappeared. Then the cops and the professors up at the college started acting weird. The new mayor, too. Night classes. Evening press conferences. At some point, there were enough of them to just take the town. They did it all in one night, after that. The winter solstice, y'know? Longest night of the year."

The wind seemed almost chilly as it whipped around the convertible.

"How many are there?"

Parker shrugged. "No idea."

"My friends. My mother. What happened to them?"

"I never met your mother. And I haven't seen Willow or that other guy since before that night."

Buffy winced, hurt by his ignorance. She wanted so badly to know what had become of her friends. But Parker could not help her.

"How far does their influence extend?"

"I heard they've turned the governor. But that's just the beginning of the king's plans for the state. Same as he did here, he's gonna turn officials and people in power, then build up enough of an army to take the whole state at once. Right now it's just around here. Sunnydale's like ground zero, with maybe thirty square miles in his control. He's smart about it, though. Keeps other towns functioning, even has people in some of them thinking nothing's changed, not even knowing the vampires have taken over. Morons. The leeches keep reproducing, though. It's only a matter of time."

His words chilled and infuriated her.

"Those people, the ones you gave to the vampires, who were they?"

Parker swallowed loud enough for her to hear it. He twitched a little. "They're . . . like me. We play along, we live pretty good. But we all have to take turns going to the lair. They . . . use us. Drink, whatever else they want. One night only. Then they throw us back until it's our turn again."

Bile rose in the back of Buffy's throat and her stomach convulsed. She nearly threw up right there in the car. Her nose crinkled with her distaste. Then she remembered something else he'd said.

"King."

"What's that?"

"Camazotz has them all calling him 'the king' now? It wasn't enough being the god of bats?"

Parker actually chuckled and shook his head. "You really have been away, haven't you, Buffy?"

Buffy frowned. "What the hell's that supposed to mean?"

But he did not answer. The evening had darkened the eastern sky to a bruised purple, though to the west it was still a baby blue. Minutes left before true night.

Ahead was the intersection with Royal Street, which ran alongside the north end of Hammersmith Park, a quarter of a mile from her mother's house. The light was yellow.

Parker began to slow down.

"Don't stop."

But he only smiled. Alarmed, Buffy turned to see a gray van speeding up behind them.

"Go!" she snapped at him.

Up ahead, a second van barreled down Royal Street. Its brakes squealed as it came to a shuddering halt, blocking the way in front of them. The van behind them slewed sideways, preventing them from retreating.

Furious, Buffy shot an elbow into Parker's side, then punched him in the side of the head. The car was hemmed in front and back. Resigned to a fight, wary of the encroaching dark, she grabbed her bag and leaped up to stand on the seat. Her hands went into the bag and withdrew the crossbow, nocking a bolt into place. She shot a glance at Parker and saw that he was groggy, but conscious. He reached for the steering wheel and the gearshift.

With a grunt, Buffy kicked him in the head and he slumped over the wheel. The car horn began to blare incessantly.

Ahead of her, four vampires in silver suits climbed out of the van. Three others emerged from the vehicle behind her.

Seven. She'd faced worse odds.

The sky seemed to grow darker in the space between one blink and another. It seemed to Buffy that eyes stared ominously down at her from the windows of every building around her. She thought of her mother's house, so close and yet impossibly far, and tried not to think of what she might find if she dared go there.

On the corner was a coffee and doughnut place she and her mother had been to a hundred times. Its familiar presence seemed almost to mock the way she knew the world *should* be. The nineteen-year-old soul that shared a double existence with its older counterpart inside her retreated even farther within.

"Come on!" she cried, outraged, prepared to tear down this ugly new world and rebuild the old, even if she had to do it alone.

The four vampires in front of the Mercedes started toward her. Buffy laughed darkly and shot a crossbow bolt at the one in front. It exploded into a burst of dust inside its silver suit, and the suit crumpled to the ground, empty. Buffy had nocked another bolt into the crossbow in an instant.

Then the vampires began to remove their goggles and hoods. It was dark enough now, and it was as though they wanted her to see them, to realize that they did not fear her. She might kill them, they seemed to be saying, but she was in enemy territory, surrounded now, and with more on the way.

Buffy fired again, but this time the vampire that was her target moved swiftly, dodging the bolt.

She nocked another one, prepared to fire as one by one they removed their hoods. With a harsh intake of breath, she recognized two of the vampires in front of her. One was a female with green-dyed punk hair, face covered in garish, red and white greasepaint. The other was an ugly male who seemed always to accompany her. Though Buffy did not know their real names, during their skirmishes—years ago—she had come to think of them as Clownface and Bulldog.

They knew, she thought. *Knew where I was, all along.* It could not be coincidence that of all the vampires in Sunnydale, these two were the ones who had caught up with her.

Out of the corner of her eye, Buffy caught motion behind her. Alert, ready to defend herself, she spun to see that the other three had also begun to approach her. They had already removed their hoods and goggles.

She knew them all.

Blond, bubbly Harmony had been in her high school class. The dead girl waved almost shyly, a sweet, stupid grin on her face. But Harmony did not worry her. It was the other two that made Buffy curse out loud.

Spike and Drusilla.

Willow sat in her dormitory room amidst a circle of white candles, their flames casting a sickly yellow glow upon the walls, flickering shadows of things that had no form. It was dark outside, but clouds blotted out the stars.

Something prevented her from summoning Lucy Hanover. For more than an hour she had tried. Now she bit her lip and fought the despair that threatened to overwhelm her.

"Lucy, please," Willow whispered into the seething shadows. "I need help. You're the only one who might have answers. Please."

With her heart and soul she reached out into the dark, into the spiritual ether she had mentally touched several times before. Something cold touched Willow's back, and she flinched in fear and shock.

"Lucy?"

As one, the candles blew out, smoke wafting up from each of them, glittering in the dark. The tendrils seemed to reach out to one another, to twine into a web of smoke, to spin and weave together into a hideous shadow face, a snarling, horned thing whose eyes seemed like endless black pits.

"Noooooo . . ." it groaned with pain and anger.

Though the windows were closed, a sudden wind rushed through the room and the smoke dissipated. Willow shivered as the temperature dropped precipitously. She blinked, searching for some sign of that malevolent presence.

Lucy was there, hovering half a foot above the ground. Her spectral form seemed even more faint than ever, a ghost of a ghost. Willow whispered her name and the spirit smiled weakly.

"I am here, friend Willow," Lucy said, her otherworldly voice quavering.

"What was that?"

"The creature was a soul-eater. My will proved too strong for it, but it has been thwarting my attempts to reach you. It attacked me here on the Ghost Roads, in the moment just before The Prophet showed the Slayer the future. I fear that it may not have been coincidence."

Willow slumped over, one hand over her mouth, and squeezed her eyes shut. Only for a moment, though. Then she stood, determined, and faced the ghost.

"You've gotta help me figure out what's going on," she said. "Ever since that night, Buffy's been all wigged. At first I thought maybe she was just pushing us away, that she was gonna go all Lone Ranger, take Camazotz down herself and get Giles back."

Something rolled over in Willow's stomach and she shuddered.

"She hasn't even tried, Lucy. I live here. I see her. She goes to half her classes, and she's looking over her shoulder all the time, paranoid, like any second, hello, ambush! But she's the Slayer. She gets ambushed all the time. Comes with the territory. And not usually during the day. It just isn't like her."

Willow paused, a chill creeping through her. When she looked up, she saw the phantom of the dead Slayer gazing dolefully down upon her, swaying slightly in the dim room.

"Lucy?"

"Where are your friends? Do they agree?"

"Definitely. It's been two days and Buffy hasn't done anything about Giles, so we're going to do it ourselves. Oz is tracking down the ship, and Xander and Anya are getting some weapons from Giles's apartment. We're going in tonight to save him, with or without her."

"Of course I will aid as best I can," Lucy agreed. *"But what of Buffy? Your words have given rise to a terrible suspicion. I think it best we find her and put that suspicion to the test before even attempting the rescue you have planned."*

Willow hesitated. A whispered voice in the back of her mind told her that it was already too late for Giles. But she would not listen. She was determined to find him and bring him back alive. The last thing she wanted to do was to wait another day.

"We're going in after Giles in the morning," she said. "I don't know what to do about—"

A key rattled in the lock. The door opened, and Buffy walked in. Willow's breath caught in her throat as she saw her friend stiffen, a dark look spreading across the Slayer's face.

"Buffy," Willow whispered.

"No," Lucy Hanover said, her voice like a breeze rustling through the trees. *"That is not Buffy Summers."*

Willow shot a glance at the ghost, then back at the doorway. She shook her head, not understanding. Buffy shot the gossamer spirit of the former Slayer a hard look, then smiled grimly.

It was the smile that convinced Willow.

"Oh my God."

Buffy crossed to her bed, bent down and reached beneath it, and retrieved a duffel bag. Willow could only stare at her, frozen with shock and grief.

"It is The Prophet," Lucy said. *"Whatever she is, the creature has taken Buffy's physical form."*

The Slayer began to open drawers and throw clothes into the bag. "It was foolish of me to think I would be able to stay here. Though it would have been more convenient, it is simpler to start over."

Willow could only stare as she zipped the bag, but as soon as The Prophet began to move toward the door, she moved to block the way. Fear and disbelief were supplanted within her by a kind of anger unlike anything she had ever known. She shook her head, jaw clenched tightly.

"You're not leaving," Willow said. "Not until you bring Buffy back."

A brittle, severe expression settled upon Buffy's face, and Willow wondered how she could not have noticed the change in her best friend. This thing in front of her was not Buffy.

"Move, witch."

Willow glanced once at Lucy, hoping that the ghost would have some way to remove The Prophet. But the specter only floated, a soul-haze and nothing more. She could not help. Willow swallowed hard and begin to inscribe arcane symbols upon the air with her fingers. Her lips moved silently as she mouthed a spell that would lock them all in the room.

With a guttural laugh, The Prophet backhanded Willow, who staggered backward and slammed into her desk before crumbling to the floor.

Dazed, she dragged herself to her feet.

But the door hung open, and The Prophet was gone. Buffy was gone.

And if Willow did not catch up with her, she might never know what had truly become of her best friend.

The car horn kept blaring. Parker, unconscious, was slumped over the wheel and Buffy could not spare even a moment to slide him off.

Spike and Drusilla.

"Well, well, Dru, look what we've got here," Spike called happily, preening like a rooster as he took a few steps toward the car. His hair was longer now, almost shaggy, giving him a more feral aspect. "That little Summers girl, isn't it? I thought she was a house pet now. Soft little kitten."

Drusilla's mad eyes widened and she made tiny

scratching motions in the air, then licked her lips. "Ooh, I love kittens. We know just what to do with kitties, don't we, Spike?"

There was bloodlust in Spike's eyes. "Oh, we certainly do, pet. We certainly do."

Harmony stared at Drusilla. "You don't hurt kittens. Tell me you don't hurt kittens."

Dru seemed shocked. "Only when I'm hungry. I'm not a monster."

It took Buffy only a heartbeat to calculate the odds. These three behind her, three more in front. Parker's Mercedes was hemmed in on both sides. Six of them. She'd killed six at once before. More than that, in fact.

But not *these* six.

Harmony and the stranger wouldn't be a problem. But Buffy knew from experience that Clownface and Bulldog were tough enough. Spike and Drusilla, though, that was the final nail.

I'm not ready. Not now. The world had changed and she had to find her place in it. At the same time, she knew that another world awaited her in the past, a place . . . a home . . . where she was desperately needed. She had to return there.

What had she told Faith, so long ago? The first rule of slaying: *Don't die.*

Once the decision was made within her, Buffy acted in an instant. She ratcheted around, fired a crossbow bolt at Spike. He snatched it out of the air, and then glared at her as though his feelings were hurt.

Buffy dove across the unconscious Parker, who slid off the horn. She popped open the door, then used her prodigious strength to shove him out onto the pavement. Her bag dropped onto the seat beside her with the crossbow, and she reached into it for one of the stakes she had made.

The vampires saw that she intended to flee, and rushed at the car.

"Dammit, Buffy! I never took you for a coward," Spike snapped at her. "I'm disappointed."

Buffy slammed the Mercedes into reverse and floored the gas. Spike and Drusilla had learned to be fast. It was part of the reason they had stayed alive as long as they had. They split up, each diving out of the way of the car in opposite directions.

Harmony stood frozen behind the car, her mouth open as though she were somehow offended. The Mercedes slammed into her, drove her back with all the horsepower the engine had. The car crashed broadside into the van with Harmony in the middle. There was a sickening crunch and she screamed, a shriek so wild and agonized that it seemed to be tearing her throat apart.

Buffy spun the wheel to the right in order to avoid running over Parker, dropped it into drive, and floored it again. Spike and Drusilla had gotten up and were rushing at her from either side, but the tires spun under the Mercedes, laying a black rubber patch on the pavement, and the car lurched forward, away from them.

Behind her, Harmony tumbled to the ground, the

top and bottom of her body only connected by torn flesh and a crushed spine. Her upper torso twitched as though she were having a seizure, but her legs lay still.

In the rearview, Buffy caught a glimpse of Spike and Drusilla running to their van.

The Mercedes raced around to one side of the van in front, but the other three vampires were there already, coming for her. Buffy lifted up the crossbow in her right hand, targeted the one she did not recognize, and fired even as he leaped toward the car. The bolt found its mark and the monster dusted, orange-blazing eyes the last to disintegrate.

Buffy tossed the empty crossbow into the backseat as Clownface jumped onto the hood of the Mercedes at the last possible moment. Then Bulldog leaped onto the trunk and tossed himself into the backseat. The Slayer swore loudly.

Her right hand gripped the stake that lay beside her.

With all her strength, she stomped on the brake.

Clownface sailed off the hood and rolled onto the pavement, even as Bulldog was thrown into the front seat. The pug-faced vampire slammed his head against the dashboard, but struggled to right himself.

Buffy punched the stake through his heart and he imploded, scattering dust all over the upholstery.

She accelerated again. Just as Clownface was getting up, Buffy ran her down. The car rocked as she drove right over the vampire, and then she was away, leaving them behind. Spike and Drusilla gave chase in the van, but they had no hope of catching up to her. Not in the Mercedes.

Clownface wasn't dead. Buffy knew that. But three out of six wasn't bad for a girl who was only trying to get away. *Maybe I should have stayed,* she thought. But she pushed the idea away. *Priorities.*

A few miles and a left turn out of view, and she had lost Spike and Drusilla. As she drove through the darkness, streetlights flashing across her face, Buffy kept an eye out for other gray vans, or any vehicle that might try to get in her way.

She had gotten away, but she wasn't free. Not until she had traveled beyond the area Camazotz controlled. And Buffy had a feeling that was not going to be easy.

CHAPTER 4

The houses on Redwood Lane reminded Buffy painfully of the neighborhood where she had lived during high school. Perfectly groomed lawns, a smattering of trees—though none of them redwoods—and a minivan or SUV in every driveway. She had abandoned the Mercedes three blocks away, and as she skulked along from house to house, it unnerved her how silent they were. No loud voices, no radios. The few lights inside barely showed through the curtains and shades drawn across every window.

Six miles from the center of town, and still no one dared breathe loud enough to attract the vampires' attention.

Halfway down the block, Buffy paused in front of an imposing Spanish-style house, and put her back against the stucco just beside a side window. From within, she could just barely hear a television set. In the driveway sat a Volvo sedan, maybe three or four years old.

She hesitated only for a moment. Then she slipped around the back of the house and across the patio to the rear door. A heavy wooden door, not a glass slider. That was good. Less noise.

Buffy kicked the door open and the three locks on it splintered the frame with a tearing of wood. It crashed open, the sound echoing out into the night. She only hoped that, locked up tight in their homes, no one would hear it.

"Oh God, no!" someone cried within the house.

Buffy rushed through the kitchen and into the living room where a haggard looking couple in their late forties cowered in a corner by the television set.

"How . . . we didn't invite you in!" the man shouted, panicked.

They thought she was a vampire.

"No," Buffy said, both hands up as she approached them. "Just sit tight, right there, and I won't hurt you. I swear I won't. Cooperate, and maybe I can even get you out of here."

They stared at her as though she were mad.

"Where's the phone?"

"What do you mean out of here? You're not trying to leave, are you?" the woman said, horrified.

"You *want* to stay?" Buffy asked. "Where's the phone?"

"On the wall in the kitchen," the man said. "You passed right by it. But please don't talk to anyone like this on our phone. They'll hear you. They'll think we're involved."

Buffy had already started back toward the kitchen, but paused at his words. She turned to stare at him again.

"What do you mean 'they'll hear'?"

"They listen," the woman replied.

With a sigh, Buffy shook her head. "Of course they do. Can't have anybody spilling the blood-soaked beans, now, can we? Still, they can't listen to every phone twenty-four hours a day. They've got you scared 'cause you never know when they're listening.

"Look, it doesn't matter anyway. We'll be gone by the time anyone can get here." She regarded them closely. "I'm Buffy. What are your names?"

The couple exchanged a tired, frightened glance. The woman stood up first, followed by her husband, but they kept their distance.

"I'm Nadine Ross. This is my husband Andrew."

"Nice to meet you. Sorry about the door. Come into the kitchen." Buffy led the way, and the Rosses followed. "Have a seat," she said, gesturing toward the breakfast table. They slid chairs out and stood gazing at her anxiously as she picked up the phone.

There was a strange clicking sound before the dial tone.

Buffy stared at it for a second. Of all the phone numbers she knew by heart, most of them would be useless now. Her mother's. The numbers of all her friends in Sunnydale. But there were two others, one that she had used only a few times, and another she had never even dialed, yet she knew both of them by heart.

The first was a Los Angeles number. Angel's number. Holding her breath, Buffy dialed, but the number was out of service. She closed her eyes and held the phone against her forehead.

Where are you, Angel?

"Please," the woman whispered behind her.

Ignoring her, Buffy dialed information for Los Angeles. She asked for the number for Angel Investigations, but the operator said there was no listing under that name. Wesley Wyndam-Pryce? Again, no listing. Cordelia Chase?

Unlisted.

As disappointed as she was, this last bit of information fanned a tiny spark of hope in Buffy's chest. It might be unlisted, but Cordelia had a phone number. Somewhere in this insane world, someone she knew still lived.

Buffy thumbed a button on the phone to disconnect, then waited for a new dial tone. There was only one other number she might call for help. It was a long sequence. Time might have caused part of it to change. Given that she had only memorized it, but never used it, she feared that she might have gotten it wrong.

Her chest rose and fell more quickly as she punched in the numbers. She felt the eyes of the peo-

ple whose home she had invaded, and she shifted un-
comfortably under their fearful, accusing gaze.

Somewhere on the other side of the Atlantic, a
phone began to ring. Buffy let out a shuddering
breath of relief as the tinny sound reached her ears.
There was a click as the call was answered.

"Yes?"

The voice was British. Buffy had never heard such
a welcome sound.

"This is Buffy Summers."

A pause, a harsh intake of breath. "That isn't
funny. Who is this?"

"Who the hell is this?" she snapped, angry and
frustrated. "Put Quentin Travers on the phone!"

Another pause. "Dear God, it really is you, isn't it?
My name is Alan Fontaine, Miss Summers. Quentin
Travers is dead. Where are you?"

"Behind enemy lines and headed south," she said.
"Can you help?"

"Hold on."

She heard a muffled sound and assumed he had put
a hand over the phone. Dull voices could be heard,
and a moment later, Fontaine came back on the line.

"Do you know Donatello's? An Italian restaurant
just off your one-oh-nine freeway?"

Buffy thought about it, found a vague recollection
of the place. "I think so."

"That's the border. We can have an extraction team
waiting for you there. One hour."

One hour, Buffy thought. A smile spread across

her face. One hour, and then she could begin to make sense of this insane world, this horrid future.

"If I'm not there it means I'm dead," she replied. "Oh, and this line is bugged. There could be a Welcome Wagon there waiting for me and for your team."

"One hour," Fontaine repeated. "And Buffy?"

"Yes?"

"I'm glad you're alive."

He hung up, and before she could do the same, Buffy heard a series of rapid clicks on the other end. Though she knew there was no way the vampires could monitor all calls at all times, a dreadful certainty filled her that they had listened to at least part of *this* call.

One hour.

She hung up the phone and turned to the Rosses. They flinched, and would not meet her gaze.

"Keys to the Volvo. Now."

Andrew Ross shook a bit as he stood to face her, face growing red. "Just a goddamn second. Maybe you scare me. Hell, you kicked in a door with three deadbolts in it. But I'm not just going to hand you my keys."

"Are you kidding?" Buffy asked, amazed. "I'm not going to leave you two here. You're coming with me."

"They'll kill us," Nadine hissed, scandalized.

Andrew crossed his arms defiantly. "We're not going anywhere."

Buffy gaped at them. After a moment, she shook her head in astonishment. "All right, look, I'm not going to make you come. The last thing I need is to wrestle with people I'm trying to help. And maybe you're right, maybe you're safer here until the nest is destroyed. But I need your car, and I'm taking it.

"Now, keys."

"They'll . . . they'll think we helped you," Andrew stammered.

With a sigh, Buffy strode across the room and decked him. She pulled the punch, but it would leave a hell of a bruise. Andrew moaned as he sat up on the linoleum. Nadine just stared at them both.

"*Now* they won't think you helped by choice. I don't have time to be nice. Give me the keys."

Nadine hurried across the kitchen and picked up her purse, rifled through it and dug out a key ring. She tossed them, jangling, to Buffy.

"I'll be back," Buffy told them.

The couple only stared at her, Nadine with her purse clutched defensively in front of her and Andrew on his butt on the floor, one hand over the rapidly rising welt on his face.

"What's wrong with you people? I want to help."

"No one can help," Nadine whispered.

"This is helping?" Andrew snapped. "You can go to hell."

"This *is* hell," Buffy told them grimly. "And I've already stayed too long. I'm outta here."

She went out the front door and loped across the lawn to the Volvo. As she drove, Buffy tried not to think about the Rosses and the fear that kept them from even trying to run away. Her destination, Donatello's, was about nine miles away. If the vampires were listening, they knew where she was headed. The only advantages she had at the moment were that they did not know what she was driving, and that she knew the roads. There were half a dozen ways to get where she was going.

The hard part was going to be guessing correctly which one of them would get her there alive.

After high school graduation, Xander Harris had retreated to the basement of his parents' house and a series of dead-end jobs, not because he could do nothing else, but because he was burdened with a depressing ambivalence. He just had no idea what he wanted to do next. All he did know was that he did not want to sit in another classroom as long as he lived. And, while hanging out in the cramped, damp space he called an apartment while his parents battled it out upstairs was not his ideal living arrangement, it had a certain charm in the area of personal finance.

Still, he knew there was more for him to do in life. It was only that he could not figure out what that might be. Thinking about it made his head ache, but once he started, it was impossible to turn the flow of thoughts off. *Ironic,* he thought, given that his girlfriend was curled up naked under the sheets, half asleep with her head on his chest and one leg thrown over his torso.

"Mmm," Anya purred.

Xander sighed. Between his general dissatisfaction with the way his life was headed and the fact that despite her vow to rescue Giles, Buffy hadn't done a damn thing to get him away from the demon Camazotz, he could barely concentrate on Anya. Buffy was acting so weird, that they were all going to go after Giles tonight, to rescue him themselves. He and Anya had even done a little old-fashioned trespassing at the ex-Watcher's house to gather up the weapons they'd need.

It's not fair, he thought sullenly.

His eyes fluttered closed. Anya snuggled up closer and Xander felt himself at last begin to relax. Though he knew Willow and Oz were due in the next hour or so, sleep seemed to be his only escape from the confusion and worry that plagued him.

Bamm! Bamm! Bamm!

His eyes snapped open and he stared at the ceiling for a minute, wondering if he had dreamed the knocking. Anya had not stirred at all. Then it came again, a hard rapping at the door that led out into the backyard, the door people used if they wanted to visit him. Willow was early.

Anya shifted, moaned a bit, and one eye slitted open. "Make them go away or I'll put a pox on them."

Xander smiled down at her uncertainly. "You're not a demon anymore, sweetie, remember?"

She sighed. "There are times . . ."

But Anya did not finish the thought. Xander climbed out of bed and pulled on sweatpants and a tee shirt as he went to open the door. As soon as it was open a crack, Willow pushed her way in. She had an enormous red welt on the side of her face, and a crazed look in her eyes.

"Xander, we have to find Buffy. She's not Buffy. I think she's going to try to leave town and we have to stop her."

Oz followed her at a more leisurely pace. Xander stared at Willow for a second, then glanced at Oz.

"Hey," Xander said.

"Hey."

"What's all this about not-Buffy?"

Oz nodded. "Possessed, apparently. Body thief, I'm guessing."

Anya sat up in bed, covers clutched at her throat, and glared daggers at all of them. "You are early."

Willow shot her a hard look, then rolled her eyes and looked at Xander again. "Come on. Saddle up. We're not gonna let this happen. If Buffy—or whoever hijacked her—gives us the slip, we may never get our friend back."

"Okay, okay, we just need to get dressed. But what about Giles? I mean, not that I was looking forward to sashaying into the lair of the ancient bat-god with a passel of vampires running around the place, but someone's gotta get him out."

Oz raised an eyebrow. "Sashaying?"

Willow rounded on Xander then, but there was no anger in her eyes, just fear and a lingering sadness. "Confession? Always kinda hoped I'd leak our plan to Buffy and she'd feel all guilty and go do the rescuing herself. Apparently no longer in the cards. I don't even want to think about Giles right now, Xander. I can't, because then I'll remember how I'm thinking, hey, he's probably dead, and I can't handle that grief. It would paralyze me, you understand?"

It was as though, with Buffy and Giles out of action, Willow had just stepped right up to the plate. She was in charge, all of a sudden, and Xander was surprised with how all right with that he was.

"Poor Giles," Anya said. "It's Buffy's fault, you know. If she hadn't been all high and mighty—"

"*If* Giles is still alive, we have to pray he lasts until morning," Willow went on. "Whatever this thing is that's taken Buffy over, Lucy Hanover is following it. Following . . . her. Right now, that's our priority. We're going to find a way to expel this thing out of Buffy. You and Oz may have to hold her long enough for me to do the spell, but—"

Xander held up a hand. *"Un momento,"* he interrupted. "Some evil spirit is holding the reins on Buffy's Slayer-powered figure, and we're supposed to hold on to her."

Willow shot him a withering glare.

"Just checking," Xander added quietly. "Wouldn't miss it, personally."

On her way south, Buffy passed through Citrus Beach, a tiny, trendy little hamlet with a single block of bistros and shops frequented only by the wealthy and their parasites.

In that respect, it had not changed.

As she drove along the strip in Citrus Beach, Buffy slowed the Volvo and peered out the window. The sidewalks were swarming with nightlife, packs of drunken Kakchiquels, their trademark black tattoos gleaming as headlights splashed across them. They sat in outdoor patio dining areas at the bistros, served by human waiters, many of whom had wide, terrified eyes, though others only looked numb, shell-shocked. The vampires roamed the streets in packs like Mardi Gras revelers, crying catcalls at passing cars.

It wasn't just vampires, either. For each clutch of undead, there were humans as well. Men and women who fawned over the Kakchiquels or gazed at them like obedient lap dogs. Buffy spotted a man on a leash, his head shaved bald, clothed only in ragged blue jeans and garish, obscene tattoos that had been etched into his skin, presumably by his masters.

Amongst the throng she spotted several demons as well.

I should stop, she thought. *These people . . .*

The thought dissipated. *First rule of Slaying.* Buffy gripped the wheel tighter, her knuckles whitening, but she kept driving, even accelerated. Several of the Kakchiquels hooted at her as she passed, beastly vampire faces on display for the world to see. Buffy flashed back to the others of their tribe she had known, the grim, silent, deadly killers. These were nothing like the others, and she wondered why.

Questions. Too many questions in her head.

A pair of blond, female vampires clad in tight, red

leather pants and matching tops began to move into
the street ahead of her. There was menace in their
gaze and their stride, and Buffy had to speed up and
swerve around them. She checked the rearview mirror and saw one of the twins make a gesture, but they
did not pursue her.

Even so, Buffy did not slow down.

Now, more than ever, she wanted to put Sunnydale
and Citrus Beach and the Kakchiquels behind her.
The lights of the town flashed across her face, but
soon she traveled into darkness again. The road
wound south, away from Citrus Beach.

I'll come back, she thought, a silent vow to everyone still alive behind her.

It wasn't long before she came in sight of Freeway
109, but Buffy did not dare go that way. More than
likely, the Kakchiquels would be waiting to ambush
her there. Instead, she said a tiny prayer she would
not get lost, and took a left onto a secondary road she
thought would eventually take her, in a roundabout
way, within a quarter mile of her destination.

For several minutes, she drove in silence, not even
the radio for company. The smattering of neighborhoods and gas stations gave way to trees on both
sides of the road. A gentle rise curved around and
through the thick woods, and Buffy became alarmed.
She did not recall a forest on this road and she could
not afford to become lost.

Keep going, she told herself. *South. Just get out of
here. A few more miles.*

The Volvo crested the hill. The road curved again as it began its descent on the other side. There were a few homes in amongst the trees, but these had lights on inside. She was not out of their territory yet, but those lights gave her hope.

The headlights washed over the trees, then the road straightened out. In the darkness far ahead, three cars were parked at odd angles, blocking the way completely.

"Dammit," Buffy whispered, there in the glow of the dash.

Instinctively, she reached out to shut off the headlights, but stopped herself. It was too late. They would have been watching for her, would have seen her coming long before she had noticed them. Her mind whirled. The Kakchiquels must have set roadblocks up along every route south. They were a couple of miles from the restaurant where she was supposed to meet the extraction team.

Her foot came off the brake. Almost before she knew what she was doing, Buffy floored the accelerator. Her seat belt was cinched tight, her hands gripped the wheel, and she aimed the nose of the Volvo right at the point where two of the cars ahead met grille to grille.

Don't die! an alarmed voice cried in her mind.

Working on it, she silently replied.

Vampires popped up from behind the cars. Doors opened and others stepped out. From the forest around the roadblock, others appeared, moving slowly down toward the road. Buffy's fingers flexed on the wheel. The headlights seemed to grow brighter, silhouetting each one of them, and the engine roared as she built up speed.

Buffy grinned.

She was doing better than sixty when the Volvo crashed into the roadblock. Buffy was thrust forward, the seat belt grabbed hold, bruised her, broke a rib, then the airbag erupted into her face and pushed her back against the seat. There was a screeching of metal like nothing she had ever heard, a shattering of glass as the Volvo rammed through the two cars, battering them aside, crushing at least one vampire.

The Volvo's bumper was caved in, scarred, twisted metal thrust down, punctured the tire. It blew, and the car slewed to one side, then flipped. Buffy struck her head against the driver's side window hard enough to break it as the Volvo rolled toward the tree line, and for a moment, she was unconscious.

When her eyes fluttered open she heard shouts of pain and fury. Her ribs hurt, and it felt as though someone had hammered a nail into each of her temples. She squeezed her eyes shut, then reached up to wipe the blood from her face. It was a surprise to find that the car had come to rest right side up. The airbag pressed her against the seat, but she reached out, clutched a large shard of glass, and punctured it.

As she looked out through the shattered glass, the vampires began to cluster around the ruined vehicles they had used for their roadblock. It was steel and fiberglass carnage. The headlights of the one car that was mostly intact shone in oily sparkles off the gasoline that seeped from the other two ravaged cars. The Kakchiquels seemed stunned for a moment, as though they had no idea how to proceed.

Then, among them, Buffy saw a pale, raven-haired creature rise up, gossamer gown fluttering around her.

Drusilla.

Perhaps thirty yards separated them. The others were dazed, but in a moment, they would come for her, surround the car, drag her out. She counted at least a dozen. If she didn't move quickly, by numbers alone they might have her.

Her chest hurt with every breath, but Buffy built a wall between herself and that pain. There was no time for it. With the shouts of the vampires in her ears and the ghostly image of Drusilla rising from the wreckage burned into her mind, Buffy released her seat belt and lunged for the canvas bag that lay on the floor. Her fingers closed around the strap and she tried to pop open the door.

It was jammed shut from the crash.

She swung the bag out the broken window, then climbed out, tiny shards of glass pinpricking the backs of her legs. The wound she had gotten in her side while fighting August earlier that day—it seemed like forever to her now—tore open again.

"Smell her, puppies!" Drusilla cried in her singsong voice, hoarse with desire. "Like cinnamon and nutmeg. A fox hunt, now! A taste of her boldness to the first to make her scream, but save the eyes for me!"

Buffy shuddered, but would not look away from Drusilla's crazed, wide-eyed gaze. They thought she was going to run away.

No more running.

Instead, Buffy strode purposefully across the pavement toward them. The vampires had begun to lope toward her, but they paused in confusion when she did not flee. Even Drusilla cocked her head sideways, where it lolled as though broken.

"What's this?" the lunatic inquired in a childlike voice.

"This?" Buffy rammed a hand into the canvas bag and pulled out a road flare. "This is for Kendra."

She ignited the flare, then threw it skittering across the pavement into the pool of gasoline that spread across the road beneath the cars and around the feet of the vampires. There was a heartbeat when nothing happened, and all eyes turned to the blazing flare.

Buffy sprinted toward the tree line.

With a sound like an enormous flag flapping in the wind, the gas ignited into a sheet of flame. Vampires screamed as the fire engulfed them. Then the first of the gas tanks exploded, and the force of it thumped through Buffy's chest like the thunder of fireworks on the Fourth of July multiplied a thousandfold. She was thrown off her feet into the undergrowth at the edge of the woods, where she kept her head down.

The other two cars exploded in quick succession

and blazing chunks of their frames struck the pavement all around. Buffy felt the heat even through her clothes, and her arms felt as though she had been sunburned. She bled from dozens of tiny wounds, and ached as though she'd been worked over good.

But she was alive.

Buffy stood up, glanced down in surprise to find the canvas bag still clutched in her hand, then surveyed the conflagration in front of her. Most of the vampires had been incinerated already. On the other side of the inferno she could see four or five of them running up the road in the other direction.

Sudden motion, much closer, caught her eye. In the midst of the blaze, burning wreckage all around, Drusilla twirled in a mad ballet of fire, her arms flung out like a little girl, her head back. The vampire's hair had been scorched from her head and her entire body was in flames, yet she danced and giggled in a high, wild, disturbingly beautiful voice.

Then she burst into a swirling tornado of burning embers, ash and charred bone fragments . . . and then she was only dust, spinning still, blown about and then drifting across the night sky like confetti.

"For Kendra," the Slayer whispered.

Buffy turned and ran up into the trees, still headed south.

CHAPTER 5

The inside of Oz's van smelled like pine trees. When his band, Dingoes Ate My Baby, had a gig, he usually ended up carrying either the rest of the band or a lot of their equipment back and forth. Not one but three cardboard air fresheners hung from the dashboard to combat the smell of sweaty musicians and beer.

Willow liked the pine scent. It comforted her, the way anything about Oz did. He was not a big guy, not a particularly strong guy, but he was resolute as stone. She had no doubt at all that he would always be there to watch her back.

As Oz drove toward the Sunnydale bus station, Willow glanced at him from time to time. In the soft glow from the dash, his face was expressionless as always, but his eyes were alive, intense and filled with a fierce tenacity. Simply having him there with her made Willow think it was all possible. They could save Buffy.

They had to.

Anya and Xander had been silent in the backseat, but now Xander shifted forward.

"Where do you think she's headed?" he asked.

Willow shook her head. "I don't know. If we knew who she is . . . what she is . . . but we don't. And we've run out of time for research."

"Does it matter where she's going?" Anya asked. "It's almost ten o'clock. There can't be many more buses leaving tonight. The L.A. express, the airport shuttle, and probably one to Las Vegas. There's always one to Las Vegas. For the gambling and carousing."

Slowly, Willow turned to regard her quizzically.

Anya shrugged. "I've left town in a hurry once or twice."

"But you came back," Xander said softly, and slipped an arm around her.

As the lampposts above the bus station parking lot came into view ahead, Oz leaned forward and killed the headlights. He braked, and pulled to the curb before turning the engine off.

"How are we doing this?" he asked.

Willow took a calming breath, a bit unnerved by her sudden, unwanted promotion to leader-girl. Buffy was supposed to be the boss, Giles the strategist. *But they're not here,* she told herself. *It's on you, now.*

Self-conscious, she reached up to gingerly touch

the bruise on the side of her face where this not-Buffy had struck her. It hurt far more than had the older, fading bruise where her best friend had accidentally hit her days before. Willow wondered why that was, but thought she knew. This new one ached deeply, all the way down to her heart.

Another breath, as she forced the coming moments into a semblance of logic in her mind. Lucy Hanover had appeared to them while they were doing research and told them that the thing that had hijacked Buffy's body had come to rest at the bus station, where she now sat waiting for her bus to arrive.

"We have to assume that Buffy . . . that she didn't take off in the few minutes Lucy's ghost was with us. If she's still there, inside the station, I'm going to try the spell from the parking lot, out of sight of the windows. Anya's going to help. It may be that she'll sense me trying to drive her out. That's where you guys come in," Willow said, glancing from Oz to Xander and back. "If she runs, you have to stop her. Keep her down long enough for me to finish the spell."

Xander cleared his throat. "But you said 'cause you don't know what this thing is, you're not even sure it's going to work. What happens if it doesn't?"

Anya smiled at him. "Well, you two will be brutally thrashed, of course. This thing has all of Buffy's gifts as the Slayer. On the bright side, though, Willow and I will think you both incredibly brave."

Xander did not smile in return. "I'll try to remember that during the thrashing."

For a moment, the four friends seemed to take a collective breath. Then, as one, they slipped out of the van as quietly as they were able and started off toward the bus station. The parking lot was far too well lit for them to simply walk across it without drawing attention to themselves. A chain link fence ran the entire perimeter.

Xander was in the lead, and he paused and gestured toward the fence. "We'll have to go around," he whispered. "Anybody notice, no buses? That's a good thing, I think."

The bus station was bordered on this side by a corporate office complex. The drive that led up to the darkened buildings had lights as well, but they were far enough away that the four of them were able to slip along the outside of the chain link fence in relative darkness. They went all the way around to the back of the station, then climbed the fence and dropped down in the parking lot. The rear of the station was plain brick, unbroken by windows, with only a rear exit door Willow thought was likely for maintenance use.

Out in the open like that, the lights of the lot spotlighting them, she felt exposed and vulnerable. With a bag of items she had collected from her own stash and Giles's apartment, she sprinted across the lot toward that rear wall. The others followed quickly. As they reached the station, the ghost of Lucy Hanover appeared suddenly among them. In the glaring overhead lights, the phantom of the dead Slayer shimmered, barely there, as though her form had been woven with spiderwebs.

"She's still here?" Willow asked.

"Indeed," Lucy confirmed. *"She awaits within, anxious and angry. I believe that she can feel me watching."*

Willow stood before the ghost, aware that the others would not come closer. Though they rarely mentioned it, not even Xander, they were always deeply disturbed by Lucy's presence.

"Whatever happens now, we wouldn't even have gotten a chance to save her without your help," Willow said. "Thanks."

"I wish I could do more," the specter whispered in her eerie voice.

"Stand by. You might get your chance. If we can drive her out, it's going to be up to you to make sure she doesn't try to invade anyone else."

Lucy nodded wordlessly and simply hovered there, the solidity of her form wavering as though the breeze disrupted it. Willow turned to her friends, smiled encouragingly, then set her bag down gently. As she reached in and withdrew the contents of the bag, she glanced up at Oz and Xander.

"Go around to either side. Just be ready. But don't pass by the windows. Don't give her a chance to see you."

They complied without another word. Willow was tempted to kiss Oz once before he went, for luck, but he was gone too quickly for her to act on the impulse, and she dared not call him back. Instead, with Anya and the ghost watching over her, she laid out the contents of the bag carefully. A small ampule of white rose oil had made it intact, despite the jostling the bag had taken. Willow daubed a bit of it on her forehead, throat and wrists, then gestured for Anya to do the same.

Quickly as she could manage, she took a small cone of black construction paper and set a piece of incense within it, then repeated the process four times. Willow drew a power circle around herself, and a star at its center, then placed the incense at each of the points of the star. With a deep breath, she sat cross-legged at the center of the circle and glanced up at Anya.

"Go ahead and light them," she said.

Anya complied quickly, using long wooden matches to set fire to the paper the incense was in. The tiny blazes flared up quickly, the paper burning, and the incense in each began to smoke.

"Wormwood," Lucy Hanover observed.

"Artemisia," Willow corrected, using a more modern name for the herb in the incense.

"What you attempt is dangerous, friend Willow," Lucy cautioned. *"If you do not know the name of the spirit you are trying to draw forth, you may succeed only in drawing it into yourself rather than simply expelling it from your friend."*

Willow paused.

"You didn't tell us that," Anya said, suddenly alarmed. "We should have used a different spell."

"Yeah, with all that extra time we had for research," Willow replied dryly.

"But . . . what if that happens? If this thing comes out of Buffy and into you, nobody else is witchy enough to get it out of you."

Willow was touched by the girl's concern, particularly in light of Anya's tenure as a demon. But she had no satisfactory answer.

"If it possesses me, Buffy will go rescue Giles and he'll figure it out."

"Not if he's dead," Anya muttered.

Willow shushed her, closed her eyes to calm herself, inhaled the fumes rising from the artemisia burning all around her. "Infernal power, you who carry disturbance into the universe, you who have intruded upon the flesh of the living, I call you forth."

As instructed, Anya scattered powdered lodestone around the circle.

"Be you *exurgent mortui,* shade, or demon, leave your somber habitation within living flesh and render yourself back unto the spirit world," Willow continued.

Anya lay a branch of hazelwood upon the pavement, pointing from the magick circle toward the brick wall of the station. The smoke rising from the burning incense seemed to pause in the air, and then to flow as one in a line along the path pointed by the hazel branch.

"Render yourself back unto the spirit world," Willow repeated.

As though it were her will alone and not the power of the spell, she could feel the magick prodding Buffy's body. In her mind's eye, she could picture the inside of the bus station as though she were truly seeing it herself.

The incense smoke is invisible now, but inhabited by the spell Willow had cast, and it works against Buffy's flesh, into her mouth and nostrils and eardrums, circling like tentacles around the thing that has possessed the Slayer's body.

Buffy tenses. Her eyes snap open.

Outside, under the glare of the lampposts, Willow stiffened at the center of the magick circle. "Uh-oh," she mumbled.

"Uh-oh?" Anya demanded, alarmed. "What's uh-oh?"

Both of them glanced over to where Lucy Hanover had been observing them, but the ghost was suddenly gone. Willow had known she would be, for in that last moment she had felt Lucy trying to help her push the invasive entity out of Buffy's body.

But they had failed. The thing had sensed her, and pushed back.

"Come on!" Willow snapped.

Anya was right behind her as they ran around the side of the bus station just in time to see Buffy—or whatever wore her body—slam the door open hard enough that the glass in it shattered. Xander was there, only a few feet away, and he leaped at her. Guilt surged up within Willow, for Xander had been badly injured only days before.

Still, they had no choice.

"We have to help him," Willow said.

But it was too late. Buffy hit him once, twice, then spun and kicked him hard enough that Xander sailed off the concrete walk and into the parking lot. Oz came running around the front of the station then, but there was nothing he could do. Nothing anyone could have done. Willow had known from the beginning that if her spell failed, they were lost.

"We're not going to just let you take her body and leave!" Willow shouted angrily, tears beginning to well up in her eyes.

The thing that was Buffy froze, turned and looked at her, almost kindly. "I have no choice," it said. "And neither do you. Try to restrain me, and I shall kill you all."

The half-dozen other people who had been inside the bus station stood just inside the panoramic plate glass window now, watching the action unfold. Willow looked from Buffy's face to the people inside. She could cast a glamour on them later to make them forget. For now, she couldn't think about what they might see.

"If I can't stop you, I can hurt you," Willow said, wiping at her eyes. She prayed now that pain might drive the thing out.

With a single gesture, her moderate magickal ability amped up by the adrenaline rushing through her, Willow caused all of the broken glass to levitate off the ground. A flick of her wrist sent the hundreds of pieces scything through the air at Buffy, who dodged what she could, and screamed as the others sliced into her.

The beast that lived in her now glared at Willow

with red-rimmed, furious eyes. "If you had walked away, you would have lived."

"That wouldn't have been living," Willow said, fighting back the fear that rose up in her then. She felt the presence of her friends around her. "Take her down now, or we've lost her forever."

Together, the four of them rushed at Buffy.

With a loud pop, all the power in the bus station and the parking lot went out. The lot was cast into darkness, the building's interior dark as pitch. Shouts of alarm came from the travelers inside. Willow and the others all faltered, keeping their distance in a rough circle around Buffy in a bizarre standoff.

"Will," Xander began, "did you—"

"Not me," she said quickly.

"Somebody cut the power off," Anya added.

Oz moved toward Willow, still keeping his eyes on Buffy, just as they all were. "Or blew the transformer out on the street," he suggested.

Inside the bus station, people began to scream. They all glanced over to see blood spattering the plate glass. Motion drew Willow's attention off to the left, and then all around.

A band of vampires swarmed across the parking lot toward them. Others slipped slowly out of the bus station, hands covered with the blood of the dead travelers.

"No!" Buffy snapped, exasperated. "What have you done?" she sneered at Willow. "He has found me."

"Indeed," came a slithering voice from within the darkened station. "I have."

With the dry whisper of ravaged wings that beat uselessly at the air, a creature Willow knew must be the bat-god Camazotz stepped out into the lot. He pointed at Buffy with a long, tapered claw.

"She's mine. Kill the others."

Buffy crouched in the darkened interior of an abandoned gas station and peered across the street at Donatello's Italian Restaurant. The place was all white stucco, glass, and brass, the sort of place where local high school kids might have their prom if their class was small enough. It disturbed her to find that the restaurant was open for business.

She had broken into the gas station almost twenty minutes earlier and found cobwebs gathering in the darkest corners. The cooler at the front was still packed with soda, and the racks under the cashier's counter still loaded with candy bars.

There were no looters in Kakchiquel territory.

Yet the place was dark, not even the hum of electricity to indicate that it might come alive again. Buffy suspected it might be used to refuel now and again, when the vampires needed it. But like so many other businesses in the region they had laid claim to, its owners had either been murdered or had fled. This close to the edge of things, Buffy suspected the latter.

And it was close, indeed. Donatello's was perhaps two hundred yards up the road, and the taint of the undead had not yet fallen upon it. *Creepy and strange,* she thought. Parker had said the vampires' expansion had been methodical, but this brought it home to her more than anything else.

As Buffy watched, late dinner customers emerged from within the restaurant. Even across the distance, a seemingly unbridgeable gulf between them, she could hear the echo of their laughter like a cold blade knifing into her gut.

Though she had somehow managed to combine the two personas within her, the two spirits, the two Buffys . . . there was no denying that there were indeed two. To the older Slayer, who had spent so long as a prisoner, that glimpse of normalcy was the first hint of happiness she had seen in more than five years. To the younger Buffy, it was a painful reminder of all she had lost by being thrust into this dark, malevolent future.

It drew her with a magnetic allure. Her heart ached to be across the invisible barrier that marked the border of Kakchiquel territory. The temptation to simply run for it was enormous. But she had told the Watcher on the phone that she would wait for the extraction team he promised to send, and she knew it was sensible to do just that. Particularly given the half-dozen cars parked on either side of the road between the abandoned gas station and Donatello's.

Though she could not really see into the interior of those ominously silent vehicles, cigarette embers burned inside three of them, and there were at least a dozen vampires that stood sentry around the cars, watching for her. Even a conservative bit of mathematics gave them more than twenty against her one, and she suspected that if she tried to cut around the intersection by diverting behind buildings and into a neighborhood, they would have scouts on the lookout for her there.

It didn't matter. They had heard the phone conversation. They knew she was coming here. Knew that the opposition was coming to bring her out.

At some point.

Another hour passed and Buffy's patience crumbled. Carefully, she slipped out of the darkness of the gas station and ran in a crouch to the silent gas pumps. It had brought her only a dozen yards closer to her goal, but that was something. In a minute or two, she was going to take the crossbow and makeshift stakes out of the canvas bag in her hand and walk right down the middle of the street toward the restaurant.

When the momentum that was tugging at her, the yearning to be free, could not be put off for one more second, she stepped out from behind the pumps and began to sprint.

They were slow. She had counted to nine in her head before the shouting began, before the car doors opened and more vampires leaped out. She had been too conservative. There were enough that she could not count them with a simple glance, and she was going to have to fight them hand to hand. All of them.

Should have waited for the extraction team, Buffy thought.

But it was too late, and she cursed herself for her impatience. She had been through too much to have it end now over a stupid mistake, her own impatience and arrogance.

Not the first time they've gotten me into trouble, she thought, as her younger self recalled her conflict with Willow and Giles only days before, and yet also many years before. Days, years, were one and the same. *No, not the first time. But maybe the last.*

On the other side of the street, the driver's door of the last of the cars opened and Spike stepped out. A lit cigarette dangled from his mouth. His face was misshapen, the countenance of the vampire within him, and in contrast to the furious rage of the others who scurried around preparing to fight her, he walked calmly away from the car, his jacket flapping behind him.

The others had swords, axes, some even had guns in spite of the vampires' usual distaste for such things. Spike was empty-handed. Dead, face as pale as his bleached-white hair, he seemed to drift along the street toward her like the scythe of the Reaper himself, gliding toward her.

Spike raised a hand and the rest of them froze, waiting for his command. He took a long drag from the cigarette and then flicked the ash away.

"You killed her." Spike did not even look at her as he spoke.

A bitter taste in her mouth, Buffy felt a hate rise up in her as powerful as any she had ever known. She remained silent, glaring at him until at last Spike turned to meet her gaze.

"She was dancing when she died," Buffy told him. A smile flickered at the corners of her mouth. "I thought you'd like to know."

Spike took another long drag, then glanced at a clutch of vampires to his right. "Kill her."

"But we're not supposed to . . ." one of the creatures replied hesitantly. "I mean—"

"Oh, bloody hell. Right, then, catch her, and bring her to me."

They moved as one, running and loping and scuttling toward her, a pack of wolves and vermin. Buffy stood her ground, lifted the crossbow, and dusted the foremost from twenty-five yards away. She nocked and aimed and released twice more, killing both her targets, before they were too close for the crossbow.

It clattered to the pavement as they swarmed her, and she pulled the stake she had brought from the rear waistband of her jeans. This was it. Five years of shadow-boxing and private *kata,* of exercise and anger.

Buffy began to move. They came at her and she flowed in a dance of death, kicking and thrusting and spinning, using their numbers against them, drawing them close to keep the others away, slaughtering them in a cloud of their own ashen remains. Gunfire erupted and a bullet grazed her shoulder. Warm blood spilled down her back, but it did not slow her. A sword point punctured her side, just below the rib cage, but she was fluid, in motion, and its owner was dead before he could harm her any further.

Then Buffy had the sword. The stake was forgotten. The sword flashed and vampires died and she choked on their floating, snowflake flesh, the nuclear fallout of slain undead. It stung her eyes and forced her to hold her breath.

Another gunshot.

A bullet through her back.

A club across the back of her head.

Buffy staggered. Fell to her knees, the sword wavering in her hands.

Spike stood over her, an ax in his hands. "So much for the not killing you thing, eh?" he asked sweetly. Cigarette firmly clenched in his lips, its tip flaring bright, he snarled at her. "Your turn now, Buffy. Let's see if you dance."

The others all stood back, but none of them dared to challenge his action. Dazed from loss of blood, Buffy was still able to make a rough guess that she had killed over a dozen of them. That was good. That was something.

But it was not going to keep her from breaking the first rule of Slaying. Spike raised the battleax, and Buffy knew she was about to die. The blade gleamed in the moonlight and somewhere nearby, probably from the parking lot at the restaurant, she heard the echo of several people, normal humans, shouting in alarm at the grotesque, macabre tableau being played out in the street.

But they were on the other side of the border. There was nothing they could do.

The blade fell toward her. The other vampires seemed to pull back even one step farther. There seemed to be more of them now, as though others had arrived, reinforcements.

Buffy tried to lift the sword.

Spike grinned.

Then his eyes went wide and his lips dropped open and the cigarette fell end over burning end from his mouth. His body jittered a little bit and he dropped the ax and stumbled toward her. Buffy aimed the blade of the sword at him and it sliced right through his abdomen, impaling him.

"Kill them!" the vampires screamed.

That woke Buffy up. *Kill who?*

She shoved the moaning Spike away from her and struggled to stand. The Kakchiquels closest to her attacked. Though she was wounded, slowed, still she spun and decapitated the nearest one, who exploded into dust. With an elbow, she drove a second back. The third grabbed her from behind, began to choke her, then he too began to jitter madly.

This time she felt the surge of electricity pass from the vampire and into her. The shock made every muscle in her body contract and ache, made her eyes go wide and her teeth feel like she had just bitten through aluminum foil. The vampire went down at her feet, and Buffy looked up to see a grim-faced man standing before her with a taser gun. A long crescent-shaped scar striped the left side of his face, cutting into the bristly stubble on his chin. His black hair was too long, hanging as a curtain that nearly hid his eyes.

It had been this man who had saved her.

"Thank you," Buffy rasped as she shook off the electrocution.

He shocked the fallen vampire again, blue electricity arcing from the weapon into the Kakchiquel on the ground. As he did, this grave, scarred warrior shook the hair back from his face and regarded her with an urgency in his sad eyes.

"We need to go," he said.

Buffy froze, staring at him, not breathing. Joy and grief clashed within her as she recognized the man.

"Xander," she whispered. "Oh my God. Xander."

"We need to go," he replied sternly, not even a flicker of a smile.

Though she bled now from so many wounds, she stood tall, held the sword up and ready, and nodded at him. "Let's go, then."

The vampires were all around them, but they were being driven back by other men and women with taser guns and crossbows. Their numbers were deteriorating even as Buffy followed Xander . . . this sad, brooding man she had once known . . . in a run for the invisible border. In the parking lot of the restaurant, she now saw a pair of black sedans and a military troop carrier that had not been there before.

Engines roared, headlights flashed, and more cars came racing down from the north, from vampire territory. They slewed sideways and bat-tattooed Kakchiquels with orange, jack-o'-lantern eyes burning, piled out with weapons in hand.

"Go, go, get the Slayer to safety!" snapped a commanding female voice behind her.

Buffy turned, saw the extraction team still fighting, but now withdrawing. The command had come from a woman with long red hair tied in a ponytail. The lithe woman raised her hands, gestured madly in the air, and cried out something in Latin that Buffy did not understand. Three vampires within several feet of her turned to glass and another member of the team shattered them all.

Her voice still echoed in Buffy's mind.

"Willow," she whispered to herself.

"Come on!" Xander snapped, grasping at her arm.

She shook him free, staring at the back of the extraction team commander. The woman turned, then, and Buffy saw her face. Willow Rosenberg at twenty-four, determined, very much in charge. When she saw Buffy looking at her, she grinned.

Buffy grinned back.

But then the newly arrived cadre of Kakchiquels rushed into the fray, and Willow's attention was back on the fight. One of them was Clownface, white greasepaint ghostly in the dark. Buffy went to go back, to help out, but Xander grabbed her with more strength than she would ever have imagined.

"No. We're not here to win. We're here to get you out."

For a long, last moment, Buffy watched. Willow set a pair of vampires on fire simply by touching them. Then she screamed out a name Buffy knew.

"Oz!"

From the midst of the melee came a sudden howl that made the hairs on the back of Buffy's neck stand up. Amidst the vampires, one of the members of the team changed in an instant. In the confusion, Buffy had not noticed him. Now there was no mistaking that it was him.

The werewolf raged, its black snout glistening, its ears twitching, teeth gnashing at the air as it charged at the approaching group. Clownface was in the lead and the werewolf rose up on its hind legs, grabbed the vampire, and tore her head off.

Oz? Buffy thought, horrified by how savage he was. The beast within him had been set loose at Willow's order, though the moon was not full.

He began to attack others, using powerful jaws and claws to tear into them, but then Willow shouted for them all to fall back. The extraction team complied instantly. Xander hauled on Buffy's arm, and then she was running toward the restaurant parking lot, mind spinning, almost blacking out. It was all too much for her.

Then they were at one of the sedans. Xander shoved her into the backseat, then jumped in front and started it up. Through the tinted windows Buffy watched the vampires give chase, but only for a few seconds. The team loaded into the military transport and the other sedan, and the vampires stopped as though they had also been ordered to fall back.

The passenger door opened and Willow dropped into the seat beside Xander.

"Spike," Buffy said. "Did you get him?"

"He disappeared," Willow replied. "He'll always save his own ass first." Then she glanced at Xander. "Move out."

He complied instantly, tearing out of the restaurant parking lot with the other sedan and the troop transport close behind. As they went, Buffy craned her neck to look out the rear window. The vampires who had survived were also retreating. They had climbed into their cars, both those that had been on sentry and the late arrivals, and begun to return the way they had come, as though the carnage had never happened, as though the people in the parking lot had not witnessed something horrible.

One car had not moved. It seemed aimed at them, headlights on high beam. They were several hundred yards away now, but Buffy could make out the form of a man standing in front of the car, his body silhouetted by the harsh lights, backlit so that he seemed more like a dark hole in the air than a man, like a thing of darkness painted over the face of the world.

Whoever he was, he stood calmly and watched them drive away.

Buffy shivered, there in the car, with these people who had once been her friends but whom she now barely knew. As they rounded a corner and the dark figure slipped out of sight behind them, she thought of the feeling she had had in the projection house at the drive-in. She thought of the crossbow that had been left there, just for her.

The two spirits that coexisted within her exulted simultaneously. Buffy was free. Yet somehow she felt her fear even more keenly than before, and a terrible dread was born within her.

CHAPTER 6

Willow felt frozen in place, there in the darkened parking lot of the Sunnydale bus station. She did not know if Camazotz's vampire followers had cut the power, or if the outage was simple coincidence, but she knew that in the end it would not really matter. The vampires scrambled across the lot from both sides, fifteen, maybe twenty. They were silent as wraiths. The night air crackled with menace.

The half that were nearest to Buffy formed a sort of semicircle around her, even as their master, the bat-god Camazotz, sprang toward her on cloven feet. Whatever had possessed Buffy, it was clear that the thing was running from Camazotz. Now that he had found her, the demon thing planned to destroy her himself. Buffy would die so that Camazotz could destroy the entity inhabiting her body.

Camazotz moved in to attack her. Buffy blocked his lunge, then shot a hard kick at his midsection that drove the bat-god backward.

"I came a long way to take the Slayer's body," the thing inside Buffy snapped. "Now you'll see why."

The vampires around her moved in, but Camazotz snarled at them and they moved back. The other cluster of vampires rushed at Willow, Oz, Xander, and Anya, who stood their ground, though they had no weapons at all. Xander and Oz had already been battered around by the Slayer. Even if they were fresh for the fight, and these were normal vampires—which, given their tattooed features and blazing orange eyes, and the way their bodies seemed to spark with energy, they most certainly weren't—even then the odds would have been against them.

With a single, muttered word and a wave of her hands, Willow drew upon the heat in the air around her, and a wall of fire suddenly blazed up from the pavement, a barrier of raging flame that gave the predators pause. They seemed, just then, like some species of ancient animal, these creatures who stared across the wall of flames, their flickering fire-eyes purely evil within the pitch black of the bat tattoos on their faces.

"Way to go, Willow!" Xander cried happily. "Torch 'em all!"

But she knew she did not have the mastery of magick to be able to do that. She had risked setting herself and her friends on fire with the spell she had just cast. Willow shot a quick glance at Buffy. She was in motion, kicking, punching, parrying blows, but Camazotz had already slashed her and she bled from several wounds.

No choice. They had no choice at all. Willow turned to her friends. "Run!" she barked.

"What about Buffy?" Oz asked, where he stood just beside her.

"We'll come back for her."

With that, Willow turned and ran toward the street side of the parking lot, toward the fence on the other side of which the van was still parked. Oz was right behind her, but Xander and Anya hung back a little, slowed down as Xander was by the beating Buffy had given him.

Willow glanced at Oz. "Get to the van. Start it up. Break out the weapons."

He sprinted even faster, and she dropped back to help Anya with Xander. Behind them the fire barrier had diminished and the vampires surged across, still unnervingly silent. Willow wished they would scream or make threats. Quiet as they were, the Kakchiquels made her mouth go dry and her skin prickle with cold fear.

"Willow, they're catching up!" Anya snapped, both petulant and afraid. "Some more fire would be nice!"

But Willow said nothing. It was hard for her to concentrate right now, and she needed focus to do magick. Without the van, without weapons, they would die. Simple as that. Her magick could protect them briefly, but that would not be enough. And even if she could keep them safe until sunrise, what about Buffy?

"Willow!" Anya shouted.

"Just run!" Willow replied curtly.

They were rushing along, Xander's arms over their shoulders, helping him to stay up and keep moving.

"Just go!" Xander said. "I'll catch up!"

Willow glanced at him, saw everything in his eyes in that one moment, his fear and courage, and his determination. But she knew Anya would not leave him behind, and neither would she.

Which was when Xander stopped. He simply planted his feet and pulled himself away from them. Before Willow or Anya could say anything, he had turned to face the Kakchiquels, who were closing in now. One of them, perhaps the hungriest, was far ahead of the others.

Xander crouched in a fighting stance. "Come on, then, you son of a—"

The vampire leaped on him, drove Xander down hard on the pavement. His head struck the ground with a loud *thunk* that seemed to echo in the silence. Anya screamed his name.

But Willow could not speak, could not scream. She saw them coming, smiling grimly now. Saw the one on top of Xander as it gripped his hair and dropped its fangs toward his throat. No words came up from within her, but something did, a dark anger she could barely control.

Her hands twitched, then lashed at the air as though it were the object of her rage. The vampire on top of Xander burst into flame, shrieking in agony at its immolation. Xander's clothes began to burn and he too cried out in pain as the heat seared his hands and face.

Anya kicked the vampire down onto the ground and began to beat at Xander's burning clothes. In an instant the flames were out.

"Not so quiet now," Willow said to the blazing Kakchiquel.

It glared at her, black tattoo blistering, and then it disintegrated in a puff of embers. The others who ran toward them faltered when they saw this, and Willow turned to face them, hands raised, ready for a fight. She wasn't exactly sure how she had managed to pinpoint that spell, knew she had nearly killed Xander, and was far from sure she could manage it again.

But they didn't know that.

"Come on, then!" she snapped.

Which was when the roar of an engine surged through the dark behind them. Headlights washed across them and Oz's van barreled into the parking lot.

Anya hustled Xander to the rear doors, opened them, and then helped him in. The Kakchiquels stood there, staring nervously at Willow, but then they began to inch closer.

"Willow," Oz's voice called from behind her. "Down!"

She dropped to a crouch on the pavement. Two of the vampires were struck in the chest with crossbow bolts. One dusted, but the other was not hit through the heart and grunted in pain instead, clutching at the wooden bolt in his chest.

Willow turned and ran for the van. Oz leaned out the driver's side window with a crossbow and fired again. Anya was in the other window, fitting a bolt into another.

"Go!" Willow said. "Can we just go, please?"

Oz pulled back into the van, put it in drive, and swung around just as Willow ran up toward the back. The rear door was open and she dove inside, then pulled it shut behind her.

Xander sat, face contorted with pain, leaning against the wall of the van.

"Hold on," she told him.

"Buffy," he muttered through gritted teeth. "We can't just leave her."

"We're not," Willow promised. Then she called to Oz up front. "Run them down. Get to Buffy."

"On it," Oz replied as he floored the accelerator.

The van rocked as he slammed into several of the Kakchiquels. Willow moved up between the front seats in time to see them smashed down under the van's wheels. They attacked the sides, and at least one of them managed to get on top and hold on.

The van raced toward the bus station and plowed through several of the Kakchiquels who had gathered as spectators around Camazotz's fight with Buffy.

They were not dead, but some at least were broken and out of the fight.

Oz said her name and Willow's heart broke. Her boyfriend felt things very deeply, but his expression and tone almost never revealed those feelings. Now, though, with just the two syllables of her name, he communicated all too much. Horror, grief, the desire to protect her from the scene that was playing out before them.

Willow sagged against the seats, her heart breaking.

As though they were actors on a stage, pinpointed by the headlights of the van, Camazotz held Buffy two feet off the ground, her feet kicking uselessly beneath her. One of her shoes had come off.

While Willow watched, tears beginning to slide down her face, Camazotz pulled Buffy toward him. A long, forked tongue snaked out of the bat-god's mouth and slipped down inside her throat. It was obscene, an intimate intrusion, a violent attack as vicious as if it had been a blade. The demon's tongue thrust between Buffy's lips and she choked and gagged. Her eyes rolled up in her head.

Willow and the others saw it all, a grotesque tableau before them. The van shook as more vampires attacked it. The passenger window cracked. The rear doors were dented.

Her heart was broken, but an even greater horror threatened to break Willow's spirit. For she understood with perfect clarity that they were too late. There was nothing left for them to do.

The passenger window shattered. Anya screamed as vampires reached in. Oz shot a crossbow bolt at one of them.

Willow did not even look. Her eyes were still locked on Buffy and Camazotz.

Suddenly, the bat-god's tongue began to slither back, inch after inch pulling out of Buffy's throat. The dead, scorched wings on Camazotz's back fluttered obscenely, like the wagging of a dog's tail. The orange fire that sparked in its eyes and those of its servants now seemed to blaze up all over the thing's body, as though electricity were passing all through him.

Buffy went rigid in Camazotz's grasp, as suddenly a dark, writhing, oily thing began to slip from her open lips, dragged out of her by the bat-god's probing tongue. It was an ephemeral thing, a dark ghost of boiling tar, a twitching, roiling cloud of blackness.

Willow had seen it before. *The Prophet.*

Somehow, Camazotz was tearing the entity right out of Buffy.

A pair of arms surged through the passenger window, grabbed Anya by the shoulder and by the hair, and began to pull her out. Her shoulder was slashed with broken glass and she cried out.

Suddenly Xander thrust a hand up from the back of the van and slapped a crucifix down on the vampire's arm. It smoked and burned and the van was filled with the smell of rotten meat cooking. The vampire withdrew, but there were others waiting.

Buffy hung limply in Camazotz's grasp as his tongue dragged the black thing from within her.

"We can't win this," Anya snapped. "We've got to go!"

"Not without *her*," Willow insisted. "Oz, run them both down. Camazotz *and* Buffy!"

"But Willow—" Xander began.

"She'll survive it. She has to. But it's the only way to buy us a few seconds to drag her in here."

"What if she *doesn't* survive it?" Oz asked calmly.

Willow didn't answer.

In the backseat of the sedan, Buffy shifted painfully on the seat, her blood sticky on the leather upholstery. Willow, beautiful and confident, watched her with great curiosity from the front seat.

Xander drove and said nothing, never even turned his head.

"You ran me over?" Buffy asked, stunned. A great deal of the story Willow was telling—of the night five years ago when they had tried to save her from Camazotz—stunned her. "I don't remember any of that."

Willow offered a brief smile. "You weren't yourself, Buffy. First you were possessed by Zotziloha, and then you were unconscious."

"Zotzil-who?" Buffy asked.

The sedan knifed through the darkness. But it was a darkness lit with streetlights and businesses and homes, a place where real people lived out from under the control of the vampires. Through the windshield, Buffy saw a large, ornate church ahead, its stained-glass windows gleaming in the night. It heartened her to know that there were still people who had faith in something.

"Zotziloha was Camazotz's wife. You knew her as The Prophet. She was a noncorporeal goddess entity, a demon yes, but not as evil as her mate. She fled him, but knew he would eventually catch up to her. Which was why she possessed you."

"Then he drove her out?" Buffy asked.

"That's one way to put it."

And then they captured me, and kept me locked up all this time, Buffy thought. But the other Buffy inside her had more questions, and other priorities. Throughout the trek she had made to get away from the vampires, the two personas' priorities had been the same, and it had been simple for them to coexist. Now, though, they were split again.

"I remember coming around while they were bringing me to my cell," Buffy said, her voice a low rasp. "But nothing before that."

Even as she said it, the younger Buffy within her knew that it was no longer as simple as returning to her own time. Given what Willow had told her, she knew that her spirit—the spirit of Buffy at nineteen—would eventually be drawn back to the time and the body it was supposed to inhabit. But she did not know *when.* Any day, any hour, any minute, she could not know when. This Zotziloha entity had been driven out of her that night five years earlier, and her spirit returned. But now, in this dark future, she could not simply wait for that to happen. Unless she could find a way for her displaced spirit to return to her correct time earlier, *before* The Prophet, Zotziloha, possessed her body, then this future could not be avoided.

"God, my head hurts," Buffy whispered. Then she looked at Willow. There was a hesitation between them, an awkwardness that five years apart had created. But Willow was still her friend, and Buffy knew that she had all the help she needed, the greatest ally she could ask for. "You and I have a lot of things to talk about, Will."

"Yeah," Willow agreed. "And soon. You have a lot of catching up to do, a lot for me to tell you. A lot of it bad. But at the moment . . ." she turned around to look out the windshield again. "Here we are."

The sky had been lightening as they drove, and now the eastern horizon was bright and blue. The sedan pulled into an unmarked street. A line of trees had been planted along the road. They drove along until they came to a building that looked like a hospital or office complex, the other vehicles close behind. The troop transport went past them, into a large lot beside the building, but the two sedans parked right up in front among some other cars.

"This is home base," Willow said.

Buffy stared at the front of the building. "Big operation."

The three of them climbed out of the car. Without a

word or a glance, Xander started for the building, but
Buffy and Willow hung back, walking slowly side by
side. After a moment, both women paused. Buffy and
Willow turned to gaze at each other. The Slayer was
overcome with emotion, a release of despair that she
had fought against for so long. Willow bit her lip, a
tiny smile twitching at her lips, and then the women
embraced. Best friends, too long apart, they had built
up walls around their hope that they would be together again. Buffy still felt some distance between
them, knew that it would take time for them to be
comfortable with each other again.

But this was a start.

After a moment, they stepped back from each
other. Buffy began to walk toward the building, but
paused again and glanced curiously at this woman
Willow had become.

"I know we have a million things to talk about—
you have no idea—but you know what's nagging at
me? If all Camazotz wanted was his wife back, then
why did he capture me afterward? Why bother with
me at all? He could have just killed me and gone
home. All this conqueror stuff, I mean, what does that
have to do with chasing his wife?"

Willow's eyes went wide as Buffy spoke. When
only silence hung between them, Willow lifted a
hand to her mouth as though afraid of the words that
might come out. After a moment, she shook her head.

"God, Buffy, I'm sorry. I . . . it never occurred to
me that you didn't know."

Icy tendrils of dread clutched at Buffy's heart. "Didn't know what?"

"Nobody's seen Camazotz for years. If he's still alive, he's probably as much a prisoner as you were."

Buffy frowned. "I don't understand."

The van rocked back and forth as the Kakchiquels tried to tip it over. Anya held up a crucifix in front of her broken window. Willow stared through the windshield and saw Camazotz retract his tongue. The black, viscous thing that had been pulled from inside Buffy's throat undulated at the end of the bat-god's tongue. Buffy was limp in his clutches but the thing was out of her body, at least.

Camazotz sucked the twitching black thing into his mouth and swallowed it whole. The bat-god's withered wings fluttered mightily and he threw his disgusting head back and laughed, needle teeth flashing in the starlight.

"Run him down," Willow said, stomach roiling in disgust. "Go!"

Oz put the van in drive and was about to floor it when there came a soft tap at the driver's-side window.

They all glanced that way at once, surprised by the subtle noise amidst the violent cacophony around them.

Giles stood beside the van, just outside Oz's window. He no longer wore his glasses, and his eyes blazed brightly with orange flame. He bore no tattoo on his face, but when he smiled at them, Willow saw the pale outline of fangs.

Something crumbled inside her then. "No," she whispered, shaking her head in despair. "No, no, no!"

"Giles," Anya said. "He's a . . ."

"You can't win," Giles called amiably, loud enough to be heard through the window. "You can only die. Don't worry, though. Buffy will live. I wouldn't dream of killing *her.*"

With that he turned away from the van and strode toward Camazotz. Through Anya's shattered window they heard Giles shout at the bat-god.

"Careful with her! Don't forget, if you kill her, another will rise in her place. The only way to defeat the Slayer is to cage her. If we can't send her to Hell, bringing Hell to her here on Earth is the next best thing."

Camazotz hesitated, but after a moment he dropped Buffy on the ground. Giles motioned to several of the others, who picked her up, and then they all retreated into the night, beyond the reach of the van's headlights, carrying Buffy with them.

In a moment, the van idled in the parking lot, and they were alone save for the dead travelers inside the bus station.

They had been left alive, but Willow knew it was not because the monster who had once been their friend had spared them. It was because they were an afterthought. With the Slayer a prisoner, they didn't matter to him. Not at all.

"Oh, man. Giles," Oz said, voice hushed.

"What do we do now?" Xander asked. "We are *so* screwed."

Willow began to cry, there in the back of the van, great heaving sobs that seemed to be torn right out of her. She didn't think she would ever be able to stop.

Buffy stared at Willow, eyes wide. She had never felt so cold. Of all she had seen and heard in this horrid future, this was the hardest blow of all. She bit her lip, tears slipping down her cheeks, and shook her head slowly.

"No, Willow. Oh, no," she whispered. "Not Giles."

For Willow, that night was five years in the past. And yet the pain of it still haunted her eyes. She pulled Buffy to her again, held her for a long moment. Suddenly Buffy pulled away.

"Giles," the Slayer said, wiping at her eyes. "Giles is a vampire."

Willow paused, then glanced away. "Not just a vampire," she said. "The most brilliant, most evil, most dangerously organized vampire who has ever lived. He's their leader.

"Their king."

To Be Continued . . .

ABOUT THE AUTHOR

CHRISTOPHER GOLDEN is the award-winning, *L.A. Times* best-selling author of such novels as *Straight on 'Til Morning, Strangewood, Prowlers,* and the *Body of Evidence* series of teen thrillers.

Golden has also written a great many books and comic books related to the TV series *Buffy the Vampire Slayer* and *Angel.* His other comic book work includes stories featuring such characters as Batman, Wolverine, Spider-Man, The Crow, and Hellboy, among many others.

As a pop culture journalist, he was the editor of the Bram Stoker Award–winning book of criticism, *CUT!: Horror Writers on Horror Film,* and co-author of both *Buffy the Vampire Slayer: The Monster Book* and *The Stephen King Universe.*

Golden was born and raised in Massachusetts, where he still lives with his family. He graduated from Tufts University. He is currently at work on the third book in the *Prowlers* series, *Predator and Prey,* and a new novel for Signet called *The Ferryman*. There are more than four million copies of his books in print. Please visit him at his website, www.christophergolden.com.

Everyone's got his demons....

ANGEL™

If it takes an eternity, he will make amends.

❖

Original stories based
on the TV show
Created by Joss Whedon
& David Greenwalt

Available from Pocket Pulse
Published by Pocket Books

2311-01